THE HOUSE WITH THREE EYES

To Gwen and David,

THE HOUSE
WITH THREE EYES

Best Wishes

JOHN HARDING

John

GREENWICH EXCHANGE
LONDON

Greenwich Exchange, London

First published in Great Britain in 2020
All rights reserved

John Harding © 2020

Printed and bound by imprintdigital.com
Cover design: December Publications
Tel: 07951511275

Greenwich Exchange Website: www.greenex.co.uk

Cataloguing in Publication Data
is available from the British Library

ISBN: 978-1-910996-43-0

to Ed and Soona

Zemblanity, the opposite of serendipity, the faculty of making unhappy, unlucky and expected discoveries by design. Serendipity and zemblanity: the twin poles of the axis around which we revolve.

William Boyd, *Armadillo* (1998)

1

STELLA WAS RUNNING DOWN THE LONG corridor leading to the Departure Lounge when she saw him standing on the moving walkway. He was facing the wrong way. She recalled, 'Our eyes met and there was something familiar about him so I looked back. If I hadn't looked back, I wouldn't have seen him fall.'

She stopped and waited as he moved past sprawled across two large suitcases. She said, 'Are you okay? Are you hurt?' He said nothing as he tried to scramble onto his hands and knees. She climbed across the barrier onto the walkway and grasped him by his shoulders, lugging him into a sitting position with his back resting against the larger of the suitcases. People pushed past or strode alongside glancing down at him and up at her.

Suddenly we were a couple. I should have left him to his own devices but I'm not like that, unfortunately. 'Can you try and stand?' I asked before taking hold of both his hands and hauling him upright. His face was familiar: the beak-like nose, the luxuriant white hair brushed back and upwards, the cold, predatory bird-like eyes. It was Harold Foster, the artist, I was certain. He would have been eighty years old, or so, surely?

When they reached the end of the travelator Foster began to fumble with his suitcases. 'You can't move with those great things,' Stella said. She found a luggage trolley and hauled his cases onto it. He seemed to have no idea what to do next.

'Where are you travelling to?' she asked.

'Venice, the one in Italy,' he said.

'2.40? easyJet? So am I! Come on,' she said, pushing the trolley towards the check-in counters. 'We can miss the plane together.'

It was a close-run thing. After the bag-drop we found ourselves at the end of a long queue waiting to go through Security, at which point Foster suddenly came alive and plunged past me into the throng, easing people aside murmuring, 'Let me through, my plane is boarding ... if you ... ? Would you mind ... ?

His feverish appearance, I guessed, frightened people, suggesting he was about to collapse at their feet. To my astonishment we reached the head of the queue within seconds. He then stopped, bewildered. People were removing their coats and jackets and stuffing their belongings onto plastic trays that trundled away on conveyor-belts. I prompted him to empty his pockets into a tray, along with his overcoat and belt and step forward through the scanner. Red lights flashed as he passed through and he was ushered to one side, told to take off his shoes and hold his arms aloft. As a security guard ran an electronic wand down his sides, I scooped up his wallet and watch, phone, keys and small change from his plastic tray and tipped them into a carrier bag. I then led him, shoes still in hand, away from the melee.

'It's Gate 10 and they've already boarded but let's give it a try,' Stella said striding off, Foster following her. Gate 10 was deserted but just as Stella let out an exasperated cry of, 'Damn!' a flight attendant appeared and ushered them down the white-panelled passenger tube that led into the plane. As they stepped aboard and looked out across rows of seat-belted fellow travellers staring back at them, Stella laughed, 'We made it! Unbelievable!'

When questioned later as to what happened during the flight, she would simply say, 'Nothing. We hardly spoke, although we were seated together in "priority" seats so as not to delay the plane's departure. "We've a take-off slot. You can find your own seats once we're in the air," they'd said. "Or you can stay where you are. You're very welcome to."

Airborne and free to move, I took down the carrier bags into which I'd tipped our belongings saying, 'I must give you these,' and I produced his wallet and keys, credit card folder and watch. As I handed them to him he said, 'Are they all mine?' and felt in his jacket pockets as if he was the victim of a stage magician pulling a trick.

'I'm Stella,' I said.

'My name is Harold,' he said.

I wanted to say, 'I know, you're the famous artist,' but reasoned it would have sounded crass, like asking him for his autograph.

Soon the roaring of the plane's engines and the chatter and bustle of passengers around her became oppressive. Stella rose, saying, 'I'm just heading for the loo.' When she returned, Foster looked at her as if she were a stranger. Perhaps, she thought, he wasn't Harold Foster after all.

'I think I'll find my seat and stretch out,' she said but he just stared back at her. 'I'll put our bags back up in the locker here, is that okay?' she said and he nodded. She then moved away, found an empty row of seats and curled up to sleep as the Alps drifted into view below.

That was it. In the half an hour or so that we were in one another's company, he spoke no more than a couple of words. He didn't thank me for helping him through security and making the flight. He seemed more baffled than anything else. It seemed to me that only seconds had passed before I was awakened by a female flight attendant touching my shoulder.

'I'm sorry,' the attendant said, 'Could you come forward to the front of the plane, please, something's happened.'

In the cramped space outside the plane's toilet, a male flight attendant said to Stella, 'Are you travelling with the gentleman you entered the plane with? The gentleman you were sitting with before you moved?'

'No,' Stella said. 'We were both late. I just gave him a hand.'

'We think he's passed away.'

'Passed away?'

'My colleague here leant over him a little while ago to see if he wanted a blanket,' the man said. 'He seemed to be trembling but he wasn't trembling. He wasn't breathing, either. He's since turned a strange colour. He appears to be dead but there's no doctor on board. We're just guessing.'

'I don't know what to say,' Stella said. 'I'm shocked.'

The man turned and entered the plane's cockpit closing the door behind him.

'Is anyone meeting him off the plane?' the female attendant asked.

'I've no idea. I think he's a famous painter. An artist.'

'Then someone will surely be there to meet him,' she said.

Stella turned and looked down the aisle to where Harold Foster was sitting.

'There's a blanket covering him,' the attendant said. 'Don't tell anyone about it. They'll start screaming. We'll be landing in twenty minutes.'

'I left my bag in the overhead locker. It's got my things in it,' Stella said.

'Wait here,' the attendant said and moved away. When she returned she handed Stella a carrier bag.

'I didn't mean that one. My bag's a rucksack.'

'We can't move anything now until we land. Please sit down, we're descending ... '

Back in her seat, Stella pushed the window shutter up. Far below through the wispy clouds she glimpsed Venice, a giant, brown jigsaw-puzzle set in the grey-green waters of the Lagoon.

At Venice Marco Polo airport I was ushered straight off the plane and led down cool, clean, silent corridors flanked by two airport security men. Entering a small room containing a table and two chairs I was asked to sit

14

and the door was closed behind me. Ten minutes passed before two policewomen entered and asked me to strip. They probed and prodded me before telling me to get dressed. As they left, two men entered, one a uniformed security guard, the second dressed in jeans, a soft, woollen sweater and wearing a baseball cap. He was short, his face hard and inflexible and when he smiled he revealed two rows of neat, white teeth.

'Miss Stella Butler?' he said. 'I'm Donato Berenga.' He indicated to a small badge on his belt. 'Guardia di Finanza. That's Border Police in English. I'm –'

' – I know what you do, and I can speak Italian,' Stella said. 'Could you tell me why I'm being treated like a terrorist?'

Donato laughed and shrugged. 'Are you a terrorist? It's possible. Can I see your passport?' he said, smiling. He glanced back and forth between her face and her passport photo. He shook his head disapprovingly. 'Not a good likeness,' he said handing it back to her. 'Not so pretty.'

'Pretty?'

'You said you're not related to the dead man, Mr Foster.'

'He's really dead? They weren't sure. No, I don't know him at all.'

'You boarded the plane with him.'

'I helped him because he was struggling with his bags at the airport. We hardly spoke at all after that.'

'You are not a friend of Mr Foster's?'

'I didn't know him *at all*,' Stella replied. 'How awful is this? I can't believe it.'

'Why are you here in Italy?'

'I'm studying conservation in the Lagoon.'

'Staying where?'

'The Hotel Canaletto. It's near San Marco.'

Donato's phone rang. He rose and said, 'Excuse me,' and left the room. When he returned he said, 'Mr Foster's body is being taken to Giovanni e Paolo Hospital. It's on the Fondamenta Nuove, north shore. The civil authorities would like you to go there to identify him.'

'But I can't *identify* him!' Stella said. 'I'm not a family member. I'm sure this isn't right. Surely someone must be waiting for him?'

'There's been an announcement but no one has come forward.'

'He's a famous artist, there must be somebody. He was very old to be travelling alone.'

Donato shrugged. 'You were the last person to speak to him before he died. If you come to the hospital now and answer some questions maybe that's all that will be necessary.' He rose and stood by the door. 'There will be an inquest later. The magistrate will enquire into his state of health and so on. What you say might be important.'

'Do I have to make my own way to the hospital?' Stella said.

'No one is meeting you outside?'

'No, but I need my phone to get my bus tickets and my bookings,' she said.

'Your phone?'

'I wasn't allowed to take my rucksack off the plane. My phone's with Mr Foster's things. They got mixed up in Security.'

'But you said you didn't know him?'

'It was chaos at the airport. I tried to sort things out on the plane but we didn't have time. I asked the attendants for my rucksack but they wouldn't let me go and get it. I've only got this carrier bag, which isn't mine.'

'Things will be clearer at the Hospital. Everything's going there, his bags, his body. Come, you can travel with me ... '

I left the Arrivals area flanked on either side by uniformed officers with Donato leading the way. The waiting crowd stared as we hurried past, Donato pushing people aside, which only seemed to draw more attention to us. I felt like a celebrity – smart-phones flashed and I think someone actually screamed ...

Outside, the afternoon was growing dark. The sun was shielded by low grey clouds; rain felt imminent. We reached a jetty where a large grey military-looking motor launch with Guardia di Finanza emblazoned on its side rose and fell on the gentle swell of the Lagoon. As we boarded Donato said, 'It'll take ten minutes to reach the old city,' then made his way forward to sit with the helmsman.

Once out on the water, I peered through a spray-flecked window. The clouds were pushing down on the wide expanse of water stretching away into the distance where I could just make out a faint blur of light stretching across my line of vision. Gradually, above the roaring of the boat's engine and the thumping of waves against the hull, I became aware of the sound of a phone's ringtone emanating from within the carrier bag.

Stella rummaged inside the bag and retrieved a small, unfamiliar mobile phone.

'Hello?' she said.

'That's not Harold is it? Harold?'

'Do you mean Harold Foster?' she said.

'Who else? It's his phone isn't it? Who's that?' the voice asked.

'Who are *you*?' she said but the line went dead. Before she could check the number it rang again.

'Hullo? Sorry about that, the money ran out. I'm in a phone box. What's the problem? Where's Harold?'

'Are you a relative?' Stella said.

'No. Where's Harold?'

'I'm afraid he's dead.' There was a silence. 'He died on the plane. Hullo?' Stella said.

'You must be joking! This is a wind-up, has to be ... '

'I'm on the way to the hospital now.'

'Who are *you*?' the voice demanded.

'Stella, Stella Butler. I sat with him on the plane. If you can help I'd be grateful. You can identify him.' There was another silence. 'Hullo?'

'This isn't a wind-up?' the voice said again.

'You can talk to a police officer. I'm on a police-launch now, going to the Giovanni e Paolo Hospital.'

The line went dead again. Stella tried to ring back but could only obtain a long-disconnected tone.

As we drew closer to the city, I could see people hurrying along the Fondamenta Nuove shore- line boarding or disembarking from numerous large waterbuses that churned to and fro. Our small craft slipped beneath a bridge and entered a canal that led between a jumble of buildings, boatyards and small warehouses on one side with a high brick and plaster wall on the other. I looked up into lighted windows, at heavily beamed ceilings, at faces peering down at me. 'I'm in Venice,' I said to myself, trying to convince myself that it was happening. 'I'm in Venice.'

They reached the quayside and Donato rejoined her. 'Ospedale,' he said, indicating to the shore.

'And this is Harold Foster's,' Stella said, proffering the mobile.

'Mr Foster's?'

'I explained to you before, our belongings got mixed up going through Security. I grabbed his things from the plastic trays and they got mixed up with mine in a carrier bag. I didn't realise I had his phone until it rang while we were on the boat coming here. Someone just phoned Harold on it. He's been waiting for him. So, you must take it as it's not mine.'

Donato held up his hands in mock protest. 'No, no. This isn't my jurisdiction. You must give the phone to the inquest magistrate. Or the family.'

Stella was about to protest when she saw another smaller craft pull in further along the quay with a large box straddling its stern. 'That's not Harold's body in there, is it?' Stella said, pointing to the box. Donato nodded. Orderlies in orange uniforms then appeared, chattering and laughing, and carried the box into the hospital. Donato hurried after them. Stella followed and found herself in a long, brightly lit corridor. Donato called back, 'Wait!'

She sat on a bench and rang her mother on Harold Foster's mobile. Her mother said, 'I called you earlier but you were switched off.'

Stella said, 'This is the wrong phone. It's not mine. Long story. I'm safe. I'll call you tomorrow but don't call me on this phone.'

Donato reappeared some minutes later.

'I'm sorry,' he said, 'there's been a misunderstanding. It's better if you go to your hotel. You'll be contacted there.'

'I told you, didn't I?' Stella said. Donato shrugged.

'You'll be called tomorrow, no doubt.'

'On what? Not this?' she said.

Donato smiled. His small, perfect teeth gleamed in the bright lights of the corridor as he raised his right arm in triumph. He was holding her rucksack. He then delved into one of his trouser pockets and produced her phone which he handed to her.

'Tomorrow the British Embassy will call and tell you what to do.'

'You've given my number to someone? You've *opened* my phone?' she said.

'To the British Embassy – only,' he said and shrugged again. 'I thought you would be pleased to get the rucksack. It's not, how do you say, the protocol?'

'Well, I'm really grateful. Thank you,' she said.

'And it was nice to meet you. I'm sorry for the confusion. I hope you enjoy your stay in Venice,' and he shook her hand, turned and hurried away before she could respond.

I sat back down for a few minutes, looking through my rucksack, baffled by the speed of events. I then walked out of the hospital and found myself in a large open square. To my left the façade of a huge brick church rose high into the early evening sky. Tall lamp standards were casting long shadows across the large stone flags of the square. Occasional figures hurried over a small bridge to my right or disappeared into distant alleyways away to my left. 'I'm in Venice,' I said to myself once again, as if I was a little girl. It was hard to grasp. It was as if I'd slipped in via the back door. I'd expected crowds, fuss and excitement. Instead, it felt as if everyone had gone home. But not quite everyone ...

Harold's phone burst into life again. The familiar voice said. 'What's happening?'

'Nothing's happening,' Stella said.

'I'd like to speak about Harold.'

'I can't tell you anything. I'm going to my hotel. Call tomorrow – his relatives will have this phone. You can talk to them.'

'I need to have a word with you. It won't take long.'

'I'm about to leave the hospital. I can't hang about waiting here, I really need to get on ...'

'No need to wait. You're wearing black jeans and a sort of donkey jacket, correct? Stay just where you are,' the voice said.

Moments later, Stella spotted a figure hurrying across the square towards her, a man wearing a shabby Burberry overcoat and a Stetson hat pulled down low almost obscuring his face. As he drew closer he looked up and waved.

'Stella, I very much hope!' he said. He dropped the cigarette he was smoking and stamped on it. He extended a hand. 'Keef Cottesloe. Fancy a drink?'

2

KEEF LED ME TO A TINY bar boasting a bright red door situated at the foot of a nearby bridge. It was crowded, it seemed at first glance, with old men in mufflers and flat caps and women laden with shopping bags. Off-duty gondoliers dressed in black puffa jackets and jeans pushed up against the counter drinking wine and chewing on cicchetti bar-snacks. They were shouting and laughing at the tops of their voices; it was hard to hear oneself speak. Keef found a space for us at a wooden bench in a corner of the room and ordered two glasses of red wine.

Keef was thickset and heavily built with round powerful-looking shoulders. His grey hair was tied back in a ponytail that sported streaks of an unnatural reddish colour; one ear sported a gold earring. His large oval face was dominated by a battered-looking nose whilst a goatee beard and moustache formed a greying oval ring around a tightly drawn mouth that exuded a dull tobacco smell as he spoke.

'This is a real bummer!' he said, 'How did Harold die?'

'He probably had a heart attack. He was very frail. He was travelling alone with a lot of baggage.'

'Did you know Harold well?' Keef said.

'I didn't know him at all,' Stella said. 'Did you?'

21

'I'd arranged to meet him here off the bus at Piazzale Roma, where the bridge from the mainland ends, and take him to his hotel.'

'You live here?'

Keef shook his head. 'I've a camper van on a site on the road to the airport.'

Stella placed Harold Foster's mobile phone on the table. 'Could you take this?' she said.

Keef sat back, stroking his beard with long, bony, broken-looking fingers. 'I don't use mobiles, can't afford them. I was ringing you from a call-box.'

'I don't expect you to *use* it! It's Harold Foster's. I thought you could give it to the family or whoever comes to identify him when you meet up with them. I agreed to meet *expressly* to hand it over. It shouldn't be in my possession.'

'It shouldn't be in mine, either.'

'So, you're not going to take it?' Stella said and rose to go but Keef beckoned her to sit down.

'Please, wait. A minute ... sweetheart, please.'

She sat back down. 'I've had a very long, very distressing day so far – and I'm not your sweetheart,' she said, taking a sip of wine, 'and this isn't a donkey-jacket either. It happens to be a Barbour jacket and cost me over £200.'

'Points taken. It's been some day for me, too, traipsing back and forth, Harold dying. You know who he is? Or *was*?'

'An artist, very famous, very old.'

'One of the biggest. Did you talk to him on the plane?'

'He wasn't in a talkative mood.'

Keef laughed. 'That's a good one! I mean before he died.'

Stella shook her head. 'No. Once we were on the plane, he hardly said a word.'

They both took a sip of wine and stared at one another in silence.

Stella said, 'Are you a painter, too?'

'Me? No. I'm a musician, a drummer,' and he waved his hands about in front of him, 'Bam, bam-a-bam!' and laughed. 'Ever heard of Moonstone?' he said. 'Before your time, maybe. What are you, 20s?'

'I'm 29 ... '

'Really?' Keef pulled a face.

'What's that supposed to mean?'

'Nothing, nothing. You just don't look that old. Not that 29 is *old*, mind. You wait till you get to my age. He didn't mention me, then?' Keef said.

'Obviously not, otherwise I'd have known who you were, wouldn't I? What do you want with me, Keef?'

He leaned forward as if afraid others around them would hear. 'Could I ask you a small favour? I'd appreciate it if you didn't mention me to anyone, at this inquest or whatever.'

'Keith,' she said, ' ... to begin with ... '

He shook his head. 'K*eef* ... with an F. K*eef*.'

'I'm sorry, *Keef.* Is that a proper name? Never mind. First, I hope not to be present at an inquest. Second, why would they ask me about you? Third, why all this furtiveness?'

'You're right. They'll only ask you what happened on the plane. Anything else is your own business.' He sat back.

'You must admit this is a pointless exercise, meeting you in order to assure you that I won't tell anyone that I've met you ... '

'I phoned you. On his phone, remember? You might have mentioned it. You probably already have.'

'But if you're involved with Foster in some way then I'd be breaking a law, by concealing your existence from the authorities.'

'I didn't have anything to do with Harold dying. I've been here for months waiting for him, living hand-to-mouth off next-to-nothing. I'm no danger to anyone. I'll make contact with his relatives, next-of-kin, whatever, but for now this whole thing is too big a deal. I'm asking you to do me a favour, that's all.'

'Why?'

He cackled and tapped the side of his nose and then winked. It was surprising, she mused, just how many irritating gestures he could pack into a few seconds.

'Could I contact you when you've met Harold's relatives?'

'I can't imagine I'll be of any use to you. However,' rummaging in her bag she handed him a small card. 'That's my number.'

Keef took the card and scrutinised it. 'That's friggin' handsome! Put it there, Stella,' he said, extending his hand.

'But don't try to contact me on *this* thing,' she said, putting Harold's phone back into her bag.

'You're an event organiser?' he said, looking at the card again.

'In another life. Just for now, for a couple of days, I'm a student. A *mature* student,' she said, giving Keef an unamused smile.

'Studying what? Art?'

'I might look like an art student to you, what with my "donkey jacket" but I'm actually doing a Master's degree in Conservation Ecology. I'll be taking photos for research out on the Lagoon tomorrow, at least I hope I will unless someone dies in my hotel bedroom.'

Keef laughed again and coughed on his wine. 'Good one!' he said.

'Are you here with your band?'

'No, no band any more,' Keef said. 'I'm semi-retired because of illness but I'm getting over it. I'm almost better now. I've refused to let it take me over and beat me. There are some things you can't beat, obviously, old age and all that comes with it for starters. You can't deny that. That's why I had to stop. Bad back, dodgy knees, tinnitus. You name it. I've got rheumatism in my neck and shoulders. I've a headache 24/7 but I'm not going to complain because that was my life. I've lived hard and fast and I've enjoyed it but now I can't do it. You sure you've not heard of *Moonstone? Falling Angel? Demons and Villains?* None of those albums on your iPod?'

'I don't have an iPod.'

'You should move with the times, my girl. He then sang in a strained falsetto.

'All the women I see just remind me of you

I keep thinking I see you before me

I remember our past

Like I'm looking through glass ... '

Stella watched Keef's small mouth open displaying tobacco-stained teeth. People glanced at him from across the bar.

'That sounds like Deep Purple?' she said.

'No comparison. Purple are an incredibly heavy riff band with some of the greatest epic riffs of all time, I grant you. We're a – were a – rock band with riffs, but with *harmonies.* We always used the harmonies to lift us into another dimension, way above any other bands.'

He raised three long, deformed fingers and intoned, 'Black Sabbath – riff band. Deep Purple – riff band. Moonstone – harmony rock band. I was the driving force, the thunder above the clouds! You know what they called me? The Bear! Ladies loved me! I had a bunch of little wind-up toy bears that played drums! I used to give them away to fans. Great days! Great days ... Fancy another glass of wine?'

'I must be going.'

'A coffee?' he said. 'You could listen to some tracks – I've got some on a cassette ... battery's a bit duff but – '

'I must find my hotel. I need to get up early tomorrow.'

'Fair enough,' Keef said.

They left the bar, Keef with his overcoat buttoned up to his chin, his hat once again wedged low. At the centre of the square stood a large equestrian statue.

'D'you know who he is?' Keef said, 'On the horse? Bartolomeo Corleoni – a warlord employed by the Venice commune hundreds of years ago to do its dirty work.'

'Stand there for a moment,' Stella said as she took out her camera. The camera whirred. She pressed another button and a print emerged. Keef leant over her to watch it develop.

'Bloody hell, what's that? A Polaroid? Takes me back!'

'A modern version, Keef. You should move with the times. Here, a souvenir for you,' and she handed him the copy.

''Andsome,' Keef said. Stella noticed that he had a definite West Country burr to his voice.

'And it's Colleoni, not Corleoni. You've got your warlords muddled up.'

'That's not all I've got muddled up, sweetheart. Sorry, no, you're not my sweetheart, *I know, I know*! You're not dressed for December, either. You not freezing?'

'I don't feel the cold,' Stella said.

'Well, look after yourself, my girl. I'll call you.'

Stella watched him walk away across the square, a round-shouldered, slightly lumbering figure with a pronounced limp beneath the incongruous Stetson hat. A cloud of cigarette smoke soon drifted upwards, he turned into an alleyway and he was gone. She shivered slightly.

I consulted my phone for directions, then plunged into the nearest alleyway. As I hurried along I could hear the sounds of footsteps and far-flung voices all around me, chattering children and birdsong drifting over the roof-tops, mingling with the tolling of church bells clashing and colliding in the distance. I crossed small bridges beneath which motor launches churned dull green water into foam before gliding away, guided by silent figures standing in the sterns. I struggled to get my bearings amid the seemingly endless narrow alleyways, some ending in canals, some in bare brick walls.

I paused by a hotel whose large front window was filled by a Christmas scene populated with tiny electrically powered people twirling and tobogganing and miniature fairground roundabouts spinning to the strains of 'Have Yourself a Merry Little Xmas'. It reminded me that I must buy my mother some sort of Venetian gift before I left.

I reached a large square which was deserted but for a distant figure hunched on a small stool in front of a painting easel. In the centre of the square stood a large, circular stone block carved with figures, a well-head, a relic of the days when Venice collected rainwater for drinking. I began to take pictures of it when, out of nowhere, a small girl ran past me screaming and hurling handfuls of birdseed around her. Grey pigeons swooped down overhead before jostling on the ground around me, tumbling and fighting and crushing one another to get to the seeds. Alarmed, I waved my arms about in a futile gesture but found the birds were under my feet. I heard myself cry out and I stumbled. Suddenly there came a clapping noise and immediately the birds rose as one, scattering above me before racing away across the rooftops.

A small, stout man wearing a long black overcoat was standing close by Stella. He wore a black, almost shapeless, hat pressed down to his ears and had a round, fleshy, pugnacious face.

'Sorry about the pigeons,' he said in Italian but with a marked English accent.

Stella gave an embarrassed laugh. 'They startled me. I feel a bit stupid, screaming like that. I always thought Venice was plagued by cats, not birds.'

'No, no, the cats have all gone. They morphed into little old ladies wearing fur coats. They're lovely objects these, aren't they?' he continued, indicating the well-head, 'and worth a great a deal if you could move one of the damn things! I'm guessing you're English. Do you know Gimpel Fils, the art gallery in London?'

'I know Gimpels,' she said.

'You look like someone who might have worked there. No? What are the snaps for?'

'I'm studying ecosystems. The wells beneath these things once collected rainwater for drinking before they began pumping in from the mainland.'

The man stared at her as if not hearing.

'Are you on a painting holiday?' she said. 'You were sitting at an easel.'

'Do I look like a tourist,?' he said. 'It's this hat!' and he pulled it off to reveal wisps of grey hair. 'I was a tourist here many years ago but I never went home. I sometimes paint here in the square. The light falls perfectly on those windows up there. I'm Alex Osbourne,' he said. He then looked up at the sky and said, 'Talking of rainwater, it'll be falling on us in a moment. Do you have a few minutes? Come, I'll show you something. Don't worry, it's nothing to do with pigeons.'

He hurried back across to where his easel stood, packed it into a small wooden box before beckoning to her to follow. 'It's this way, not far,' he said, and walked off in the gathering evening shadows towards a hump-backed bridge at the opposite side of the square.

Stella followed him through a dank, shadowed alley until he stopped by a shop-front, pushed a glass door open and announced grandly, 'Welcome to my world ... '

It was an art gallery comprising two rooms connected via an archway. Elegant gilt chairs were positioned by an oval table upon which lay brochures and order forms. Lamps suspended from thin metal rods ran the length of the rooms illuminating paintings hanging on the walls. A highly polished wooden floor shone beneath bright spotlights.

'Have a look around, I'll be back in a minute,' Alex said and disappeared through a door at the far end of the room.

I stared at the paintings hanging in the first room. They were unremarkable but accomplished Venetian scenes depicting misty canals, the Doge's Palace, gondolas in the moonlight. Alex reappeared wearing a smart black homburg hat tilted to one side. He gave a wave of his hand and declared, 'Some of my work. Not that of a Sunday painter, you see ... ' and he touched my shoulder to guide me towards some quite different paintings of young women, naked but for suspenders and stockings, some seated on ornate chairs gazing into space. One girl sat at an angle so that the dressing table mirror in front of her afforded the viewer a full view of her small breasts. Each picture had the name 'Alex' written in swirling, ostentatious script in the lower right-hand corner. They looked like the sort of pictures one might see in the foyer of a lap-dancing club.

I felt conscious of Alex standing close to me, watching for a reaction. 'It's a lovely room the models are sitting in,' I said. 'That's St Mark's Square through the window behind them across the Canal isn't it?'

'My studio. It's on the Giudecca,' he said. 'All these you see were painted there. I have several canvases hanging at any one time on the walls and fragments of them appear in other paintings. The studio becomes a

continuum of interior and exterior, artifice and reality, layers of memory and evolving drama ... '

It felt as if he was trying to impress me, perhaps even sell me a picture.

I said, 'I like the bright colours. I feel a bit sorry for the women, though. They're stuck in a sort of dream-world, with that beautiful view behind them.'

'Interesting that you should say that! No one's said that before, certainly not a woman, about the dream, I mean.'

Alex was now talking in earnest. 'I'm dealing with an area of human consciousness that exists on the borders between reality and dreams.' His round, plump face was animated by a touch of eagerness and, I thought, just the faintest of smirks. He looked a little like an overfed Roman emperor. He was also, I knew for certain, flattering me. The bit about the dream wasn't what I'd meant, and he knew it.

'One afternoon when the sun was out and the light was so flat, I posed this model here against the mirror; then Venice and the studio were visible in the background and the light fell squarely on her. You see, the mirrors allow reflections of Venice itself – the Zattere and the Gesuati church – as well as occasional portraits of me at work! That's me in the corner!'

He went across to a table and picked up a glossy book. 'My catalogue. Just been printed. Have one with my compliments. Don't object! You know, you really do look just like a girl who worked for Gimpel Fils,' he said. 'Would you like something to drink?'

'No thanks, that's nice of you but I'm heading for my hotel and need an early night. It's been a busy day.'

'You've just arrived?'

'A few hours ago.'

'For the Christmas holiday?'

'No, sadly. I'm going back home tomorrow in the evening. Your gallery is terrific but I must go – '

'Seems a very short stay. A romantic break?'

'I'm going to take some pictures of salt marsh erosion, out on the Lagoon, beyond Torcello. It's research for a MA. Part-time. '

'You have a boat?'

'I'm going to hire one. I think I can do that in Burano.'

Alex frowned. 'At this time of year?'

'It was an impulse trip. I'm a professional planner but not where my own life is concerned!'

Alex took out his phone tablet and punched in a number. He waited, staring at me before someone answered. 'Ciao, Remigio! What are you up to tomorrow? I have some work for you, a client, needs a boat.'

I made to protest but Alex waved me away. 'Okay. Okay. Taking photos on the Lagoon.' He turned to me. 'When's a good time for you? 11 a.m.?

I nodded.

'Okay. Bye,' and he turned back. 'You're fixed. Remigio lives on Burano. He's a fisherman, or he is when he can get out of bed! All you need do is turn up at the Burano jetty and ask around for him.'

'I don't know what to say. Thank you very much.'

'You'd have been wasting valuable time otherwise. You must let me know how you get on.'

Just then the door at the end of the gallery opened and a younger man appeared. He was taller than Alex, dark-haired, dressed in jeans and a black t-shirt.

'This is Franco, my son,' said Alex. 'Do you see the resemblance? I'm better-looking though! He's a fabric designer. Stella's a student, Franco, ecology.'

'Fascinating,' Franco said.

'I've booked her a trip tomorrow morning with Remigio on Burano.'

Franco nodded. 'Okay.'

At the gallery door I said, 'I can't thank you enough. The paintings are great, by the way. I'll look at the book tonight. Do you mind if I take a photo?' Alex stepped back and posed, leaning on the doorframe, grinning.

'Ciao!' he called out as I hurried away.

Later, in my hotel, I showered and lay on the bed, watching as darkness finally obliterated the gaudily decorated ceiling. My room felt as if it had been worn threadbare by a thousand tourists. The gilt on the cheap ornate bedsteads, mirrors and chairs was chipped and fading; the chandelier was a grimy plastic copy of a Murano glass original. A dull smell of drains drifted in from the en suite bathroom. From my window I looked out upon a brick wall adorned with faint graffiti at the foot of which stood a derelict water pump, its basin filled with litter.

I googled, 'Harold Foster'. He stared back at me just as he had been doing some hours before at Stansted. There was nothing as yet about his death. Instead, site after site was devoted to information about him and his work: 'The finest British painter of the past fifty years'; ' ... the most celebrated European painter alive today ... '; 'an inheritor of a tradition that includes Di Chirico, Goya and Ingres ...'

It was overwhelming. Almost on cue, his phone rang.

'Keef?' I said, but it was a woman.

'Is this Mr Pictor? It's about his hotel room for this evening.'

'You must have a wrong number,' I said, and rang off.

3

THE JOURNEY TO THE ISLAND OF Burano from Fondamenta Nuove took almost an hour. Stella watched from the open stern deck of the waterbus as the old city of Venice disappeared beneath the horizon of the Lagoon. As far as the eye could see there was now just flat, flat water and an occasional abandoned island dominated by derelict, red brick buildings where seagulls perched amid rogue foliage. It seemed to Stella that the further she travelled, the wider and higher the clear blue sky became, pushing down and almost crushing the distant land masses so that they appeared to be mere faint slivers of light on the horizon.

Burano itself was accessed via a narrow waterway that led between the adjoining islet of Mazzorbo on one side and what looked like an overgrown, deserted island on the other. The waterbus glided past brightly painted houses lining the Mazzorbo waterfront, beyond which could be glimpsed tidy gardens and orchards, an all-pervading silence broken only by the sound of the boat's engine.

She was early and she wandered from the boat station along a pathway that led to the centre of Burano along a canal lined by yet more houses decorated in startling colours. The water of the canal was motionless and of the deepest green beneath an opaque morning haze. Stella stood, transfixed by the stillness, the bells of the church of San Martino pealing.

Back at the Burano boat station I waited for Remigio as small crowds of tourists disembarked and headed for the famous lace-shops and cafes, smart-phones flashing. After a few minutes I spotted a middle-aged man wearing a peaked baseball cap and braces that supported waders up to his armpits staring at me from further along the jetty. I called out, 'Remigio?' and he gave me a wave before turning to walk away. I followed.

At a nearby jetty where his boat, a dinghy equipped with an outboard motor was moored, we shook hands, but he was terse, had little to say and didn't look straight at me. There was also little room for me to sit down in the tiny craft. As we pulled away, I asked if his name, Dei Rossi, was related to the Burano house colours. He at first made no reply so I pressed on like a tourist reading from a guidebook.

'I read somewhere that the houses in Burano were painted in bright colours so that sailors and fishermen could identify their own house as they came in from the sea.' He shook his head and said that house decoration was decided by the council regulations ('norme e regolamenti') and that homeowners had to write to the authorities for a list of permitted colours if they wished to change theirs. He then shrugged and we said no more about house colours.

I proffered a map of the areas in the Lagoon where I hoped to visit and where I could take photographs of certain flora. He glanced at the map and seemed to dismiss it. 'Impraticabile, impraticabile,' he repeated, gesturing at something on the page that I failed to see.

'I want to photograph some of the areas where soil bioengineering work has been going on. It's related to a visual survey of salt marsh edges I'm doing for my college course,' I said. Ignoring my question, he spoke as if he was a tour guide reciting his lines, saying, 'Beyond Torcello is a wide sandbank full of birds,' but I said I wasn't interested in birds. 'I'm interested in salt marsh sites, ones most susceptible to erosion,' but he pretended not to understand me. He stood in the stern of the boat gazing ahead, not looking at me. Now and then as we wove through various water channels I asked him to slow down so that I could take pictures. He just shook his head and shrugged and continued apace.

I did what I could, photographing reed-covered banks as they glided by, unable to stand for longer than a minute before toppling back down, Remigio murmuring, 'Sta attento! Attenzione!' In this way time passed until we were back at the Burano boat station with Remigio shouting greetings to various colleagues on the shore. As I stepped from the boat I half expected him to say something to me but he said nothing, just glanced at me before falling into a deeper conversation with a colleague.

Something indefinable was going on but I could say nothing. His strange behaviour had been quite deliberate, I thought. If I had booked the trip myself then I would have complained or asked him what the matter was, but it had been a favour on Alex's part. When I asked him how much I owed him, he waved me away. It really was impossible. I wanted to ask if there was someone else who might take me out the next day but it would have looked rude. There was nothing else to do but return to Venice.

I sat alone in the stern of the passenger boat as it made its way back to the old city All around me the bleak swathes of motionless water no longer held the same mysterious promise as they had done earlier in the day. Clouds now obscured the blue sky and a cold wind whipped across the surface of the Lagoon. I retreated inside the boat and sat amongst the chattering women, the old men and the tourist couples, and looked at the photos I had taken with mounting dismay.

I felt like weeping. I had come all this way and I had achieved nothing at all. What was worse, I had no idea what to do next. Returning to Burano the following day now appeared pointless. As I tried to calm myself down and think, my phone rang. There was a message from Donato. I must go to the Bauer Hotel in Venice that afternoon to meet consular officials and Irene Foster-Wyatt, the daughter of Harold Foster.

Foster's death came rushing back into my mind. I'd pushed it away, tried to relegate it to something insignificant, but it would now be headline news, surely, and I was embroiled in it, somehow. I felt trapped all of a sudden, unable to move forward.

Heading to her meeting with Harold Foster's daughter, Stella found that flooding earlier in the day had made it necessary to bring out long trestle-tables covered in green matting which stood end-to-end down the middle of each main street. She picked her way gingerly along the raised, sodden surfaces until she reached the Hotel Bauer, where two shimmering silver-branched Christmas trees in gigantic tubs flanked the vestibule entrance.

At the reception desk beneath a golden chandelier she said, 'I'm Stella Butler. I'm here to see someone in connection with a Mr Foster.' Moments later a besuited man approached, introduced himself as Daniel Jones of the British Consulate and indicated that she might follow him.

Irene Foster-Wyatt was a tall woman in her fifties wearing a heavy, camel-coloured, floor-length coat and a pair of eastern-style culottes. Her black shoulder-length hair was cut with a severe horizontal fringe and she wore bright red lipstick. Her sharp blue eyes sparkled with curiosity and anxiety as Stella was ushered into the small reception room to meet her. Beside Irene stood a short nondescript man in a grey suit with thin wispy hair and a sleep-starved crumpled face.

As she engulfed Stella in a bear-like embrace, Irene murmured, 'Hullo, hullo ... I'm Irene ... ' Stella breathed in a musky, deep perfume that made her head spin and found herself lost for words as Irene continued to hold her, both hands gripping Stella's arms tightly as she stared into her face.

'It's good to meet you,' she said. 'This is Seth, my husband,' she said, indicating the small man, who nodded back.

Irene then guided Stella to a couch. They sat together and Irene took deep breaths, her eyes brimming with tears. She said, 'My father died of a heart attack. You wouldn't believe the red tape that's involved, you'd think he'd been murdered! It's all such a shock. You were with him when it happened, they tell me?'

'I helped him catch the plane. He'd fallen on the travelator at Stansted and – '

'A what-alator?'

'A travelator – the moving walkway. He'd toppled over and was sitting amongst his cases – '

'Oh my God!' Irene gasped.

'I helped him up and we went through Security together. We got into a scramble and had to run for the plane. I sat with him during take-off and – '

' ... it must have been the fall, a delayed reaction, wouldn't you say, Seth?' Irene interrupted. Seth made to answer, but Irene turned away and looked hard at Stella. 'Tell me Stella, what's your connection with my father?'

Stella shook her head. 'Connection?'

'Harold was still sleeping with a young woman a year or so ago and I thought maybe you were she. How old are you, Stella?'

'I'm twenty-nine and I certainly wasn't sleeping with Mr Foster. I – '

'You look younger. You just helped him onto the plane, is that it? Don't ask me why he was travelling here all on his own. We hadn't spoken for quite a while. I live in New York and get across to see him when I can but he lived like a hermit. He never picked up a phone and accused me of all sorts of machinations. Did he talk much?'

'We only said a few words. I felt tired and went off to sleep. They woke me and told me he had died. I was taken to the hospital where he'd been taken. They say I have to give evidence at an inquest.'

'But you never met him before bumping into him at the airport, you say? Did he proposition you?'

'Of course not. We hardly spoke at all ... '

'This is so unnecessary. You're a young girl, you have a holiday to enjoy and you're out here caught up in all this. Seth, does this young girl need to be here for an inquest? It seems a waste of her time.'

'The magistrate may want to ask her questions,' Seth ventured.

'Couldn't she just make a written statement? She sat with him on the plane, they chit-chatted until she went off to find another seat. He was okay at that point. What else can she say? She'd never met Harold before. You never met him before, did you?'

36

'No,' Stella said, 'but I do have his phone.' Stella produced it and held it out in the palm of her hand.

'His phone? Harold's?' Irene said. She took it gingerly, as if it might explode. 'Seth? Harold had a cellphone!'

'I ended up with it after the confusion at Security. Mine was in his luggage and the police retrieved it. A policeman returned it to me but wouldn't take Harold's. That's why I still have it. I'm so sorry.'

'My God,' Irene said, turning the phone on. 'It works. Why would he have a cellphone? Seth, look at this.' Irene looked at Stella. 'Nothing else?'

'I beg your pardon?' Stella said.

'Nothing else of Harold's ended up with you?'

'No, no. I gave him back everything. I'm not a thief, you know,' Stella said, feeling a rush of anger.

'There's no numbers on this thing,' Seth interrupted, looking down at the phone. 'Not a damn thing.'

Irene looked at Stella. 'It's a mystery. He never had a mobile phone, not to my knowledge. Did Harold say why he was coming to Venice? But you two didn't speak, did you?'

Stella said nothing but felt her heart beating hard against her chest.

'Didn't anyone try and contact him at the airport? Surely someone must have been waiting here for him?' she said to Seth.

'The police said there was no one waiting,' he said.

I was about to say, 'There was someone,' but it occurred to me that I would be here for ever if Irene learned about Keef. I was also annoyed at her insinuations, that I was lying about being sexually involved with Harold Foster, but the moment passed and she looked up from the phone and said, 'You're surely not on your own here? It's such a romantic city,' which annoyed me even more.

'I'm doing some ecological research, taking pictures of marsh erosion. I leave the day after tomorrow,' I said.

'So you have work to do,' she said. She turned to Seth. 'Let's get her to give a statement and have done. She's busy. Where's that embassy official?'

Seth left the room and Irene said, 'We took a flight from Newark last night. It seems an age ago. My head's in a whirl. You're very pretty. Do you use a stylist?'

Before I could answer, Seth hurried back. 'They say it's okay. They'll get a statement from her if they feel they need one.'

Irene clasped my hands. 'That's great! That'd suit you, wouldn't it, Stella? I'm going to arrange a burial immediately for Harold. I'd love you to be here for that. You were the very last person to see him alive! Can I contact you?'

I took out one of my business cards and handed it to Irene who glanced at it, then said, 'But I thought you said you were a student. It says here you're an event manager.'

'I'm taking a sabbatical. Three short days.'

'Do you speak Italian?' she asked. 'If only you could be here for the funeral!'

She rose and hugged me and I felt again the large, powerful woman beneath the flowing robes. 'Thank you for coming,' Irene said. I then found myself being ushered past the antiques and the lacquered Chinese panels in the reception area, back out into the Venetian evening.

I felt a rush of relief mingled with guilt. I had lied in a way, concealing Keef's existence. They would find there had been messages on the phone. I could say I'd used the phone because mine had been unavailable, which was true, but it would leave me vulnerable to Irene's suspicions about my role in Foster's demise. None of it would matter, though, as I'd decided that by then I would be on a plane home. The trip had been a disaster and I wasn't going to prolong the agony.

I went back to my hotel, showered and lay for a while, checking messages on my phone. The news of Foster's death had now reached the wider world and I read more about his life and status in the art world. Thankfully, there were no pictures from the Marco Polo Airport, just a couple of stills of Venice, the Biennale Gardens, a shot of one of his last paintings. It was much too complicated a story for me to relate via text to friends so I contented myself with mundane comments about the weather. I checked flights for the next day but could find nothing suitable. I decided to head for the airport first thing and hope for a cancellation.

All of which only made the feeling of disappointment that much keener and the small hotel bedroom even more claustrophobic. I grabbed my jacket and hurried out, determined to retrieve something from the wreckage. As I reached the front door, I stopped. The line of fairy lights strung across the hotel sign that hung over the entrance now cast a reddish glow – across Keef Cottesloe's grinning face.

'Oh no!' I said before I could stop myself.

'Happy to see me, then?' Keef laughed, stepping forward to give me a bear-hug.

4

'I OWE YOU SOME ENLIGHTENMENT,' KEEF said. 'Let's go for a walk.'

'I'm not interested,' I said, untangling myself from his embrace and making to walk past him. 'I've just met Harold Foster's daughter and life would have been a lot simpler if I'd been able to say to her, yes, Harold was on his way to meet an old friend, that is, you. Instead, the whole thing is now a mystery. They have no idea why he was coming here. They probably think he was losing his mind. I'm sure he wasn't but it makes no sense otherwise. And when they find out that you exist, I'll probably be dragged back into it all. His daughter more or less implied I was Foster's mistress although she badgered them into letting me off having to attend the inquest. And now you turn up again like a bed penny ... '

'Bit harsh, that,' Keef said.

'I came here to do something very simple for myself and even that's turned into a mess, a waste of time and money. The sooner I get back home the better. I'm going to change my flight for tomorrow, so no thanks, Keef.'

Keef held his hands up. 'Cards on the table, I haven't helped matters. You're right, I left you holding the baby or whatever. So, I owe you. Let me make amends. I'd feel a right bugger leaving you to sit in some *poky hotel room with all this around, La Serissima. Once in a lifetime place.'*

'It's La Serenissima. The Most Serene. Not how I feel at the moment.'

'I know a nice place where we can eat. On me. What do you say?'

I should have said no at that point and gone back up to my hotel room but everything was in a muddle. I felt disconcerted, uneasy – and lonely.

'A coffee and a walk, then I must go,' I said.

'You're on!' Keef said and he put his arm around my shoulder to lead me away.

They walked for some time in silence past empty restaurants with waiters standing outside proffering menus, past illuminated gift shops full of tiny glass figurines and cheap Venetian masks and emerged into St Mark's Square over which the cathedral loomed.

'Is this cafe much further?' Stella asked.

Keef pulled a guidebook from the bag slung across his shoulder.

'We've walked the wrong way. We shouldn't be here at all. Never fear, we'll get a waterbus and take a trip up the Grand Canal to the nearest boat station and we can leg it from there.' He smiled and winked and said, 'They used to call her Laughing Girl, but look at her now!'

'I'd prefer it if you didn't wink,' Stella said. 'You remind me of an uncle I can't stand.'

Once aboard the waterbus, they found seats in the open stern. The bus then ploughed its way out into the Lagoon before veering round to head off up the Grand Canal, past the domed Salute church, the distant shore of the Giudecca dotted with gold and silver lights, a sharply defined moon hanging low and casting a silver pathway across the water, grey as steel in the quickly failing light.

I'd never been here before but it looked so familiar. The buildings drifted by like in a dream, palazzos, churches, statues, brilliantly illuminated apartments sporting glittering chandeliers, luxury hotel lobbies opening onto landing stages lit by flaming torches, casinos and art galleries.

41

I thought of taking a photo or two but so many photographs and films had been taken of this place. there was nothing that I hadn't seen a million times over. It wasn't what I'd come here for.

The canal was busy with passenger ferries and speedboats, working craft and even an occasional gondola. At regular intervals the waterbus would slow down almost to a halt, waiting its turn to dock at stations along the way, its old engine rumbling and growling and throwing up diesel fumes from the water churning at its rear. I said, 'Let's go inside, these fumes are choking me,'

'You're a bit of a spoilsport, aren't you?' Keef said. 'You should let your imagination go a little bit.'

'I'm trying to,' I said, as our places were taken by a group of Asian tourists, their cameras flashing.

Inside, it was warm and quiet with rows of silent commuters gazing down at their iPhones. Keef, meanwhile, was rummaging in his bag. He produced a photograph that he handed to Stella. 'Clarification follows,' he said.

She saw a group of three people: a tall, angular man in his forties whom she recognised as a younger Harold Foster; a young girl with what looked like a robe wrapped around her; and a tall youth with very long hair down to his shoulders.

'That's not you, is it?' said Stella pointing to the latter.

'Sadly, yes, when I had my full barnet – and that's Harold Foster. The girl in the middle, that's Alice Casteret. It was taken a long time ago, mid-seventies when I was young and good-looking. I was here in Venice when I met my lovely girl, my sweetheart, my Alice. I'd just joined Moonstone and we were on an Italian tour spending some days here in Venice with some mates. To cut a long story short, something happened to Alice and she OD'd.'

Stella looked at the girl's unremarkable pert little face (even rat-like, she thought, but didn't want to say it) with her long, trailing jet-black hair. Behind her in the photograph, through tall French windows, she could see the Grand Canal and the Doge's Palace.

'She was living in a small apartment with Vivienne, an older woman,. And I never realised, never knew until a year or so ago, that they were mother and daughter. I never twigged.'

He took the picture back and stared at it.

'How long had you known her?' Stella asked.

'About a month. Viv and Alice came to a party we were at somewhere on the Grand Canal. Alice and I hit it off big-time. I thought she was "the one", you know what I mean? Viv wasn't too pleased but she had other things on her mind.

'Viv was, or had been, a celebrated artist's model. Vivienne Casteret. She'd been photographed by top photographers back in the fifties and sixties when she was girl and she'd posed for Francis Bacon amongst others. She was a party animal, led a wrecked lifestyle. She was unruly, a riot, it was impossible for her to allow herself not to be the centre of attention in any room, if you know what I mean. She was still good-looking when I met her but losing it. In truth, she was already an "alky" and taking too many drugs.

'Harold had painted Viv way back and they'd been lovers – well, he slept with every woman he'd painted, I gather. But Viv took him seriously and she'd come to Venice this time because she'd heard he was here. Not sure how pleased he was but she'd brought Alice along and Harold had started painting her. I got the feeling that Viv had "presented" Alice to Harold as a sort of tribute, does that make sense?

'Alice was beautiful and looked like an angel. She had long legs and dark hair, dark eyes, bit like yours, and the whitest, most delicious teeth. Harold got her to loosen her hair which she usually wore in two plaits either side like a Red Indian. Buffy St Marie-style? Never heard of her. *Soldier Blue*? Anyway, it spilled down around her shoulders and she was under strictest orders not to cut it and not to get a tan – she was the whitest white.'

Stella took the photo again wondering if she'd missed something. Keef was now in full flow.

'She was a quiet girl, but she had a rowdy sort of laugh. She'd throw her head back and sort of gurgle when she was amused. Had a West Country twang, bit like mine. We were both from Cornwall, see. When she gave out that laugh, she'd bend her knees a bit, her arms dangling by her side and sort of rock back – Ha! It wasn't the delicate, dainty hippy-chick style reaction you'd expect. I connected with that. We also shared this,' and he pulled his top lip back to reveal a gold tooth. 'Alice had one, same place. It was sort of gypsy-like, back then. She was a bit rough and ready, if you know what I mean.'

'But how did you meet Harold Foster? I don't see the connection.'

'At a party in the Palazzo Ca Dario, then owned by the manager of the Who. You know the Who, surely? Before your time again? There were all their gold discs on the mantelpiece! The Palazzo's right here on the Grand Canal. We'll be passing it soon, and I'll point it out. Lovely building. Being there was like a dream come true. It was what we all wanted. Excess! Rock and Roll! Harold was working somewhere else, I'm not sure where exactly. I got the impression he was hiding from the establishment, but he enjoyed the company of younger people and liked the buzz. He was in his forties or fifties then and already a top painter. Great talker and great drinker.'

Keef stood up and pointed to the other side of the canal.

'And there it is! That's where I was, back in the day, Palazzo Ca Dario ... '

Stella looked across at the tilted building, its façade encrusted with disks of green marble and topped by large Venetian chimneys.

Keef said, 'Monet painted it. And a curse hangs over it. Really! I'll tell you about that later. Aren't you going to take a picture?' Keef said, sitting back down.

'It was Alice who brought us into contact with Foster,' Keef continued. 'She was modelling for him, as I said, in a large place where there were painters and artists working in different studios. It was shabby but freaky, if you see what I mean, and Harold had a small studio space there. He'd stayed on after some big exhibition. The Binallea, it's called, I think. It's a – '

' – I know what the Biennale is, Keef,' Stella said.

'Right. Well, Alice was excited about being a model. She had a sort of arty disposition and liked the idea of being painted by a real artist. I think that was what spurred me on to write my songs about her. 'Falling Angel', my biggest hit, was about her. I was competing with Harold. He disliked me, hated my music and was jealous that Alice and I were making out. I asked Alice to describe what the experience was like, sitting there week in, week out. "You are giving yourself up, it's very intimate, you're vulnerable and you're there for whatever's required of you," she said. "He used to curse and swear and throw gobbets of paint," she said. "Sometimes he thought I had dropped off to sleep and he would get angry. He was a bit of a tyrant where his work was concerned."

'But then something strange happened. She went out one morning and had her hair shorn, cropped, if you like. She didn't ask anyone, didn't tell me, though I thought she looked great. Harold took one look and stormed out of the studio. "What the bloody hell did you do that for?" I asked her, and she said, "I fancied a change." Just like that. I think she just rebelled in the end, sitting there with Harold taking it all so seriously and she thought, "I'll have a laugh and cut my hair!" You see, it was that other side of her, something that contradicted what you saw. You might look at her but you didn't own her; she could shape-shift – '

'Shape-shift?'

'Yeh. She could be what you wanted her to be but only for a while. Then she'd shift. She didn't sit for Harold again. The next night there was the party in the house where Harold had his studio. We were all there. And then she was, well, she was gone.'

Keef stared out across the water. Stella waited.

'Gone where?' she said.

'Gone, as in dead. It's hard to piece the chain of events together,' he continued, 'but she was found in his studio-bed. I'd been drinking big-time along with a bunch of others and she'd slipped off. Early in the morning I was woken by our manager, Rodge, and told that there was trouble, that Alice was in a bad way. I just went into shock. When I asked what had happened Rodge said she'd OD'd and that we had to get out before the police arrived. When I kicked up a fuss, wanting to see her, Rodge got tough

45

and started pulling me about . He was a big guy so I gave in, grabbed my things and left the house. There was no doctor about as far as I could see, no ambulance, I didn't know whose place it was.

'We picked up our equipment and went straight to the train station and booked tickets. I saw Harold and Viv there, sitting in the station buffet. She looked like death warmed up. We all got on the same train but we didn't talk. We changed trains at Milan, went on to gigs somewhere else in Italy. We were always big in Italy.

'That was it. Never heard another word about Alice. It was as though she'd never existed. I assumed the worst. After that, I just threw myself into it all, the work, the touring, the gigs – we were very successful. The song I wrote for her was a big hit and it seemed to keep her alive for me. Do you want to hear it? I've got my Walkman this time,' he said, retrieving it from his bag and offering it to Stella.

'A Walkman!' I said. 'It looks like a terrorist bomb. What was that you said about moving with the times?' As we passed beneath the Accademia Bridge, the lights from restaurants illuminating the rooftops, I listened to Moonstone playing 'Falling Angel'.

Down through the years
Through the torrent of tears
When I left her she screamed
You'll forget me!
We were climbing so high
Just like birds in the sky
I can still hear her weep
'Come and get me!'

The track ended and I couldn't help saying as I handed the cassette player back to Keef, 'But you never did "come and get her". Keef, you just left her, this love of your life.'
He shrugged, nodded, and for a moment I thought I had upset him.

Keef looked older all of a sudden, as if when the high spirits fled so the flesh on his face drooped. The song was maudlin and banal, I thought, but I ought to have been kinder, perhaps, although in truth, I was tiring of his tale of seventies rock 'n' roll excess.

'Not a good decision, I know. In fact, I never came back here, to Venice. This is the first time I've been back since then, almost forty-five years! So, why *am* I back here after all these years, I hear you ask?' and he gave a rueful laugh. 'Not long to the end of the tale ... Stay awake, girl!

'Well, recently, everything's been collapsing around me, first my health, then the band fell apart. I wanted to move the old songs on a bit, add something modern to them. The rest of the band weren't interested at all, wanted to continue playing the old stuff. Christ, we were becoming our own tribute band! There were arguments and I got chucked out! Effectively, I was given the boot from my own endeavour. They even took my name off our greatest recordings, so I don't get any song-writing royalties! Those songs were about my life but they hijacked them. In my eyes, my baby's been stolen from me by individuals whose motives I question. I'd been ripped off and there were lawsuits, but I failed to secure my rights.

'So, a couple of years ago, I started to write my story, warts and all, the band, the rip-offs. I thought I'll take a load of negatives and turn them into positives. There's a publisher interested, you see, and I have this chance, this one last opportunity to write my story. But I realised I needed a central hook, something to grab the headlines. And I thought, what about the truth behind Falling Angel, my big hit?'

'The lost love of your life,' Stella said.

'Exactly. That's a good line. But to tell that part of the story, I knew I needed to see Viv, to ask her about Alice. I'd run away when she'd died – but I wrote some of my finest stuff because of her, a whole frigging album that's part of rock history. You should hear the guesswork fans get up to, trying to work out who the girl was, what the lyrics meant: "The beating wings of the angel of death" ... "petals like bloodstains" ... "the blood-red moon" ... eh?!'

Stella nodded. 'A bit like the Beatles and Helter Skelter?'

'Well, not as extreme as *that*. But I realised I was in a place where I could reveal all, the truth and, more to the point, rescue myself financially.'

'A win-win situation,' Stella said.

'Before all that came about, I used to bump into Viv now and then – she was always somewhere on the London scene, though more and more out-of-it and on the scrounge. Then a year or so ago I heard she was ill and I went to see her. I found her living in a run-down Housing Association flat in Wandsworth. How the mighty are fallen! We talked about the past but not about Alice, not at first, not until the last few times I visited when she was close to the end. Her lungs were giving out, she was a write-off. She knew what I wanted, though, I could sense it.

'One afternoon we staggered out down to her local boozer for a drink and a smoke. How she made it I really don't know. We talked for a bit and then I said, "Tell me about Alice", and she seemed to deflate – all that energy, the effort to get up and out for a brief moment of flight seemed to evaporate. "Didn't we do a terrible thing?" Viv said to me, "Leaving her?" "We all did," I said. "Including Harold Foster. With a retrospective exhibition coming up in England, with a wife and children to think about, his involvement in something as gruesome as the death of a young girl would have been a disaster. For him, once free of the place, he could deny everything. He hadn't killed the girl, had he?'

Viv said, "But I was the worst." Alice was *her* lost baby, too, her fallen angel. She'd had her when she was in her early twenties but she just couldn't handle it, a young child and living the sort of "boho" life Viv preferred. So, she'd had her fostered. An old couple down in Cornwall somewhere took Alice in. Hippy-types but good-natured and Viv never saw her again until some months before we all rolled up into Venice. Alice had absconded, run off and sought Viv out, Viv said. She didn't elaborate.

'When Alice died that night, Viv freaked out. She had a reason for running. She'd had two more girls since Alice with a bloke she'd actually married but had broken up with. If it came out that another daughter of hers had suffered a drugs overdose while in her care, then she could have lost the other two. You follow me? She'd been desperate to get back to England and out of the nightmare. She wasn't a monster – just a bloody fool. Or maybe she *was* a monster ... too late now, anyway.

'I told Viv a publisher was interested in my life-story and I said the revelations concerning "Falling Angel" and Alice would put it on the best-sellers list. She took fright and begged me not to write about it before she died, which she said wouldn't be too long. I couldn't press ahead and ruin her final days.'

'No, that would be too callous of you,' Stella said.

'Exactly. So, I waited, getting poorer by the day and then I got a message to go and see her. She was in the Brompton; someone had paid for a private room. She was drugged up and not really in the land of the living, I thought, but she recognised me when I appeared. She asked me if the book had come out and I said, No, of course not. So, she smiled, and then she said, "That's good. Because there's something else. It'll make it even bigger," she said. "Alice was Harold Foster's daughter." Bam! I thought, what a story it is *now*! But the last thing she said really *did* blow me away. She said, looking me straight in the eye, 'And Alice's still alive. She's still out there, I know it. She didn't die ... '

Stella stared at Keef, wondering what to say in response. It seemed as if the story would never end. As the waterbus slid side-on to a landing stage, he rose. 'This is our stop,' he said. 'Come on ... '

5

WE ALIGHTED AT THE CA D'ORO BOAT station and walked along the Strada Nova before turning left down a narrow alleyway . Keef said, '"Ca" is short for "casa", house, Ca' d'Oro means "House of Gold", did you know that? Need I ask?'

We reached a small restaurant situated on one side of a tiny square. Outside stood three barrels converted into small tables with no one sitting at them. A simple awning proclaimed the name La Cantina and light from the restaurant lit up the pavement outside. We entered through an old-fashioned swing door and sat at a small table close by a curtained window.

'You must be hungry,' Keef said and I realised I'd eaten nothing at all since breakfast. Keef ordered a plate of mixed cicchetti and watched me as I ate.

He said, 'So how did your day go? Get plenty done?'

'My trip to the wetlands was a disaster, now you ask. All my fault because I didn't plan things properly. I thought I could wing in and wing out but I was wrong. I wanted it to be off the cuff, but I was knocked off course from the start. That's three clichés in a row!'

'I'd say they were idioms, Stell ... Clichés are more like naff sayings. When you write lyrics like I do, you see them coming. You mustn't give up, though. Keep your chin up – idiom. Don't let the bastards grind you

*down – saying. Drink to me only with thine eyes – lyric.' He laughed again
and called out to the waiter for a bottle of Prosecco. 'Let's drink to you and
me!' he said, and we clinked glasses. 'Could we go outside? For a smoke?'*

*We sat at one of the small barrel-tables where Keef lit up, sending a
cloud of smoke up into the starry sky. 'I've a feeling your story hasn't
ended, Keef,' I said.*

'True, Stell, but the best is yet to come.'

'Idiom?' I said.

'Lyric,' he said, tapping the side of his nose.

Viv, he recommenced, had been concerned that his plans to 'tell all' in a
sensational memoir might harm Harold. Although she hadn't spoken to
him for years, she'd always been loyal to him in her utterances. After she
died, well, that would be up to me. But I had my own reasons for being
careful,' Keef said

'Something told me to watch out. My side of it, the classic album, the lost
love, was one thing. But to drag in a world-famous artist was another. I'd
just lost everything in a court battle to establish my rights to the material I'd
actually produced. I'd been wiped out by lawyers. I didn't need another
crash like that. I had to be careful. I had to work things through and be clear
that I wasn't stepping into a minefield. And another thing. Harold Foster
could be nasty. I'd read that he sometimes paid criminals to intimidate
people he didn't like. He'd arranged for paintings of his which were sold on
by their legitimate owners to disappear. He was known to physically attack
people and send people anonymous death threats. He would target people
with "poison postcards". Long time ago, maybe, but all the same, the bloke
was still sleeping with young girls when he was in his eighties, you know
what I mean?

'I'd also heard that he wasn't too keen on people writing anything about
his life. Once, he was said to have sent some mobster mates to "dissuade"
a biographer who'd neglected to ask permission. A biography he'd
authorised had so disgusted him with its murky revelations that he paid the
biographer and binned the book. You get the picture?'

51

'I get the picture,' Stella said, filling up another glass with wine.

'Viv died about a month or so after dropping the bombshell to me about Alice being Harold's daughter. I went along to the funeral. It wasn't the sort of crazy celebration she'd have wanted; there was something grim and foreboding about it all. Ever been to Golders Green Crematorium? As the coffin was trundling through to the burner they played Dancing Queen at full belt. It was supposed to have been a big laugh but it felt wrong. I walked out before it finished.

'Harold wasn't there but he'd sent a wreath. Viv had always said, "Screw all that stuff about charities – I want flowers on my coffin!" And Harold had sent her flowers.

'Despite everything, I'd been tempted to go and see him but I didn't know where his studio was and what would I have said? He'd have wanted nothing to do with the whole business, obviously. But Viv, bless her, had sorted that problem out. In her will she'd left a bundle of documents for Harold, including a letter addressed to him which she left instructions saying should be delivered to him by *me in person*! It was my big chance. It took me a couple of tries but I ended up spending an hour with Foster in a café near his studio.'

'You met Harold Foster?' Stella said.

'I told him I'd been burned, cleaned out in the courts by people suing me for doing something I had thought was legal, I'd been ripped off, my work stolen. He sympathised with me. If I'd let him know earlier, he said, he might have been able to help me. Wow!

'When I told him about my plans to write the story about Alice and her death, I said, "I'm just clearing things with you. I'm alerting you to what I'm hoping to do and asking you if you want to tell me anything." He shocked me. Instead of throwing a fit, he was relaxed about it all.

'He assumed I knew about Viv's claim concerning Alice's paternity which was in the letter I'd delivered. But nothing could be proved. The papers she'd bequeathed him consisted of things she'd written down over the years, odd scribbles, dates, a crazy diary. But they were typical of her, names scratched out, a lot of it illegible. There was nothing that would prove decisive in a paternity squabble and no birth certificate.

'But where Viv's claim that Alice hadn't died was concerned, he was adamant. "She was dead," he said, "I know that. You were there," he said, "and you saw she was dead."

'Well, that was the point, I said. I was told she was dead but then I was hustled away. There was no autopsy, no medical report, nothing official. Once I left, I never heard another thing. I didn't ask Foster what he'd been told, what he knew. As far as I knew, he'd done a runner as well.

'He seemed to think a bit, and then, out of the blue, he said, "Have you ever considered returning to Venice? You never know. What if Vivienne was right?" Which was strange. I'd not even considered it. Why go there? Everyone who'd lived there back then must either be dead or retired or moved on. I was startled he'd even given it a thought but it seemed he was curious. He said, "What a story that would make for your book ... to find her again after forty years!"

'It was something else I'd not considered. I'm a bit slow on the uptake ever since I fell off my drum-kit one night in Brussels ... I'll tell you about that some time. I said to Harold, "I'm broke, but if you give me some money for a week or so, I'll do it." And he agreed.'

'Harold Foster paid for you to come here?' Stella said.

'That's it. Gave me a few hundred quid.'

'Didn't that make you suspicious? From what you've been telling me, he wasn't a straightforward character ... '

'There was a proviso. That I tell him everything I find out and that his name isn't mentioned. He wasn't there, if you know what I mean. I said yes. It was money in the hand, Stella. That's all that mattered to me. A means to an end. Ask no questions. Well, not to him. So, I got my old camper van fixed up and set out. Couple of months go ... What an adventure! I'll tell you about that some time. Right now, I'm settled on a camping site halfway to the airport. I get the bus into Venice each day, takes ten minutes.

'When I first got here I went through the usual channels. I thought if she'd died someone must have dealt with her funeral. Her death would have been registered. Was there a grave? In spite of contacting all the relevant authorities, I couldn't locate a thing. I then tried to find people who might still be around who'd been there then. I had a couple of addresses that I followed up but nothing doing. Venice has changed. It's become a rich person's paradise, all holiday homes and rich folks' bolt-holes. The old bars have all gone. Nobody left from the old days, which could have been predicted, you might say. We're talking forty years ago.

But one night, lying in the van and ready to give it all up, I remembered a small coffee bar we used to go to. There was a young Venetian guy working there then, he'd now be in his seventies, Luigi! His name just popped up out of thin air! He'd been a great fan of the group. He loved the music, he loved Alice. And from that moment I had something to work on.

'I found the place not far from the Accademia bridge across the Grand Canal. It's now run by one of Luigi's sons. He said, "Luigi? No, he doesn't live here any more, he has an apartment on the Lido but he drinks with old friends in a bar not far from here. If you go there and wait, you'll see him. Someone will point him out."

'So, I kept an eye on the place and, sure enough, one day he came in. He didn't look a day older! I started to chat. He didn't remember me at first but the name Alice struck a chord. "Yes," he said, "I still see her around Venice. Small, dark-haired. I was gob-smacked." I said, "You *see* her? She's alive?" He knew nothing of the events of that night when we thought she'd died. I said, "Are you sure?" And he said, "Of course," and a day later, just like in a detective novel, he says, "Here," and he pushes a piece of paper across the table towards me with a name and an address on it. "It was Alice's. I couldn't believe it."

'So, you found her?' Stella asked.

'She lives an hour or so from Venice on an island called Mazzorbo, or Burano, one of those.'

'I know it,' said Stella. 'And? Have you spoken to her? What did she say?'

Keef stared at Stella for a few moments with an uncomfortable-looking smile on his face pondering his next statement. He took a long swig at his wine.

'She denied the lot. She said I was wrong, that she'd never heard of me and that she'd only lived in the region for a few years. I showed her the photo – of herself and me – and she seemed to go funny and told me to leave. I knew the moment she looked at the photo that it spooked her.'

'I'm not surprised.' Stella laughed. 'I can't believe you would spring something like this on someone! How could you be so sure it was *her*? On the say-so of an old Italian who ran a bar forty years ago!'

Keef shrugged. 'I was looking straight at her. It was her.'

'And what about the gold tooth? I'm surprised you didn't ask her to open her mouth so you could check.'

Keef said, 'You're taking the micky now.'

Stella said, 'You're telling me all this because of my tenuous connection to Harold Foster, obviously. So, if it was all a wild goose chase, why was he on his way here? Stumbling on travelators, rushing through Stansted without his shoes on, dying on the plane.'

There was another silence before Keef said, 'Because I told him it was her. I told him I'd found her. Bit of a white lie, I admit. But it was Alice. I know it was. It's a gut feeling. I saw her there in front of me.'

'Keef,' Stella said, 'Luigi's got her mixed up with someone else. Alice is not an unusual name. In any case, why are you still here? It's all over now, isn't it? Don't tell me, I know, that's a Rolling Stones lyric. But Harold Foster's dead, Vivienne is dead, the girl – your girl, her daughter, his daughter, whatever – is obviously dead. You're free to write about it and make up whatever you want. No one can contradict you. '

'It's *her*. I just need a little time. I know it's her. I'm going to meet her son.'

'Her *son*?'

'He works here in Venice. She said that if I didn't leave her alone, then she'd get him to persuade me otherwise. I said, okay, let me meet your son and that's what I'm going to do. I'm going to try and get the son to help convince her. If the son agrees that she's who I *know* she is then we could all go to see Foster's family. What an event that could turn out to be!'

Stella said, 'But you agreed with Foster to keep his name out of it. You're breaking your word. You took his money and now your reneging on the deal. And what do you mean, we? You're not including me in all this?' She shook her head. 'I'll be finished here tomorrow and far away by the time the son throws you into a canal! You're lucky this Alice woman hasn't called the police.'

'But that's the clincher. She hasn't. That's what struck me. She's afraid of something.'

'So am I,' Stella said, 'Probably of the same thing. *You!*' And she laughed again.

Too loudly, I thought, and realised I was feeling light-headed. It was always a bad sign, that sensation of becoming detached from oneself. I'd been drinking too much and listening to Keef's long story and its ridiculous conclusion. Up above, the night sky swirled ever so gently.

'What time is it?' I asked Keef. 'My head's starting to go around. I need to walk a little bit.'

Keef rose and took me by the elbow and guided me once again down the narrow alley. 'Follow me,' he said. We found ourselves wandering through a small fair in Campo Santo Stefano. Christmas lights were strung across a score of would-be wooden Alpine huts stacked with seasonal gifts: hand-thrown Venetian glass, Burano lace, Florentine paper, soaps, perfumes, gloves, scarves and wooden toys – all of which whirled round before my eyes. People dressed in overcoats with scarves wrapped around their necks stood about drinking hot mulled wine and smoking. As I watched, a Father Christmas figure on stilts ran past ringing a bell followed by small children whooping. On a stage at one end of the square, a reggae band complete with a Rasta saxophonist and trombonist started playing while a 1950s black-and-white movie was projected onto a screen behind them.

People began to dance. I clapped my hands and swayed to the music. I heard Keef saying, 'But I will say this, I play my drums with feeling. Whatever the song needs I feel it and I put it down. I've jammed with Stevie Wonder's band, Billy Cobham, Earth Wind and Fire ... '

Someone wanting to dance tugged at my sleeve. It was a tall youth, who said, 'Andiamo a ballare!' and pulled me towards him. I stumbled and almost fell. Keef said, 'Push off, mate,' but the youth laughed, grasped my arm and shouted something to some friends standing nearby.

I said, 'It's okay, he's harmless,' but Keef barged into him saying, 'You heard me, sonny. Leave her alone … '

At which point I sensed the mood change. Another youth grabbed Keef in a bear-hug and shouted, 'He does not want to fight, he only wants to dance!' and began to whirl him round as Keef cursed. I tried to pull away from the tall youth holding me as others in the crowd scattered. 'I hate silly arguments with drunken people,' I said to no one in particular, 'but I'm not one to talk … '

Moments later came a loud shout and I was pushed roughly to one side. I stumbled and heard a scream that I couldn't be sure wasn't coming from my own mouth. The images began to spin more and more swiftly: I was being held round the waist by Keef, I was laughing again and we started to fall backwards onto the pavement. Squeezed into a bundle of bodies, we lurched back up again. Someone shouted 'Avanti!' and then came the sound of a whistle blowing.

I clutched at the nearest shoulder before stumbling and scratching my fingernails against the wall of a bridge. Then came a cry, 'Run!' in English and I began to do just that, my legs like lead as I heard myself shouting 'Run everybody run … !'

I remember watching someone disappearing across a square chased by a crowd of youths; then a familiar face appeared close to mine and a hand gripped my shoulder. The moon seemed to bounce up and down on the rooftops. Everything slowed down and moved as if in a dream. There were stone steps, a boat, the sickening smell of canal water mixed with engine fumes, a wild rocking and rolling and a cold wind – and, finally, that ominous out-of-body experience of an evening's red wine rushing from my stomach up into my mouth and out like a fountain, sparkling like the lights of a thousand palaces flashing by.

6

A MOVEMENT SOMEWHERE BEYOND HER CAUSED Stella to open her eyes. Her head throbbed. She'd been lying still for some minutes straining to hear something, anything, to reassure her and give her a clue as to where she was. Instinct got the better of her. She blinked through the pain, the sharp stinging sensation as daylight hit the back of her retina.

She saw that she was in an unfamiliar room in a bed far too large for her. Standing at the foot of the bed was a small, middle-aged woman wearing an oilskin jacket that was dripping wet, her hair plastered to her head, her eyes dark and thoughtful. She was staring at Stella.

'Have I had an accident or something?' Stella said then peered beneath the sheets. She was naked. The woman moved not an inch and Stella, sensing her own vulnerability, clutched at the bedclothes, bringing them up to her chin. She smiled. The woman frowned and looked as if she were about to speak but hesitated. Stella said, 'I've no idea how I got here!' and added, 'I'm sorry, is this your bed?'

The woman shook her head and said, 'I thought no one was here.' She then turned and slipped out of the room, closing the door behind her.

Stella waited a moment before sliding out of the bed and turning the door handle. Outside was a narrow corridor lined with prints and framed pictures. The woman had disappeared.

Stella went back to the bed, wrapped the sheets around her once again and felt the room turn slowly as her hangover toiled away like some large, dark, heavy substance pushing against her eyeballs.

I was in a room with a high, stuccoed ceiling and no windows except for a skylight upon which rain was falling through grey skies. The floor was highly polished wood with rough-cut, expensive-looking rugs scattered here and there. I'd already felt their softness underfoot.

There was an ornate fireplace on either side of which stood two carved female figures supporting a shelf above which hung a small painting of a girl's face. A tall mirror in a chipped gilt frame dominated one wall of the room. My clothes were neatly piled on a chair along with my rucksack. I found my phone. It was 9.30 a.m. Flashes of the previous evening's events in the bar tormented me. What had I done? Got stupidly drunk, obviously. Who might have undressed me, who had brought me here? Who, perhaps, I had spent the night with?

Back outside the room and along the hall she found a small bathroom. After showering and dressing, Stella made her way further down the narrow corridor and reached a staircase. Descending, she glanced through porthole windows looking out upon a stretch of water across which she could see the old city of Venice. She realised she was on the Giudecca island.

The rain had ceased and the far city was now bathed in the weak morning sunlight. The campanile of San Marco rose into a sky still misted over by the morning's downpour, while to the right a short way across the Lagoon stood the bell tower of San Giorgio. Through another small, open window she felt the sea breeze coming off the Adriatic, stirring the curtains and freshening the air.

She heard music, the distant sound of a piano. She passed through a small windowless room with exposed wooden ceiling beams before entering another larger room that had floor-to-ceiling windows looking out onto the main canal. It was a painter's studio. There were unfinished canvases perched on easels plus a small wooden table cluttered with pots of paint, squeezed tubes, and used brushes. There was also a jumble of what looked at first like random objects but which Stella sensed had been carefully organised for maximum effect.

There was a seated skeleton, some vividly coloured drapery and Japanese screens, some tie-dyed parasols, some complete and some torn and, half hidden, a battered antique chaise longue. There were also old-fashioned lamps and lampshades, a boar's horn twisting up from its base, a number of miniature classical statues as well as a large globe of the world perched on an old sewing machine.

Almost hidden in one corner Alex Osbourne was sitting at an upright piano. He was perspiring, his scant hair laid in wet wisps across his forehead and he started to sing to her as she approached:

'If you ever wake up from your dreaming
A-scheming, eyes gleaming
Then if suddenly you take a screaming fit
That's it!'

He stopped. 'How do you feel?' he said. 'You look rough. The song describes you perfectly.'

'I feel disgusting and disgusted with myself. I can't remember getting that drunk since I was a teenager. I should have eaten something substantial, not just bar snacks.'

He stood and closed the piano lid.

'You weren't that drunk. The boat-trip didn't agree with you and you were tired.'

'Who brought me here?'

'You were caught up in a fracas in the Santo Stefano Christmas market. Franco wasn't too far away and recognised you. His launch was moored nearby. He brought you here for safety.'

'Franco brought me here? Your son? I have no idea what happened. One minute I was watching a band, the next there seemed to be a lot of screaming. Was I sick in his boat?'

'Over the side. Coffee?' he said, rose and disappeared down some stairs. She turned away and looked out of the windows at the Venice skyline. She retrieved her camera from her rucksack and took a picture just as Alex reappeared with two mugs of coffee.

'Taking snaps? I must get one of those. Real, hard copies ... '

'Did Franco stay here, too?' Stella asked. Alex laughed again.

'Yes, but you slept in my daughter's room. She lives in Padua with my ex-wife but it's her room to use whenever she's in the region, working. I didn't undress you if that's what you're thinking. My gallery partner, Rebecca, was here and she disrobed you. Your reputation's intact, along with everything else I should think!'

'Was it Rebecca who woke me?' Stella said.

'That would have been Maria Pasolini, the cleaner,' he said. 'Maria would think nothing of the odd female in my daughter's bed! My daughter's not gay, by the way. Is Maria still here? I must see what she wants, maybe money. Excuse me,' and he hurried away again.

I wandered about the room. Prominent on one wall was a large notice board where cuttings were displayed from the International Herald Tribune, Country Life, The Spectator featuring Alex, recounting riotous parties he'd attended, gourmet dinners he'd cooked, celebrity guests he'd entertained. The board looked as contrived as the surrounding studio with photographs of Alex as a tousle-haired young man sitting in a bar, as a middle-aged man posing as Napoleon with a funny hat, in a bar sporting a pig's snout. He also appeared as an older man leering from behind a smartly dressed woman in the foreground as well as in his studio standing at his easel and staring into the camera while a naked model posed in the background. As the years had advanced his girth had expanded and his face grown broader, fatter, his once dark hair now mere wisps across a balding pate. Yet always that smug, smirking expression, pleased with himself

I went to sit by the tall windows sipping my coffee as my hangover ebbed. The pale watery light streaming in soothed me and I closed my eyes

61

and listened as the rain recommenced, sweeping across the water beyond and pitter-pattering against the glass.

My attention was drawn to a movement close by, a door being opened and closed somewhere, someone, a woman, speaking intently, urgently. Then came a cry, then silence. Had I imagined it? I leaned forward to see if it was someone outside on the pavement below. There was no one. A vaporetto out on the Lagoon rolled and buffeted past heading for the next station.

I wondered what I was going to do with the day ahead. I was intent on going home but I needed to settle up at my hotel, then get to the airport. When Alex returned, he said, 'How did the Burano trip go?' and I was momentarily stumped.

'I meant to thank you again for arranging that. I'm really in your debt,' I managed.

'But?' he said.

'I don't think Remigio really understood what I wanted. He didn't accept any payment, either, and I must give him something. Perhaps I could give you something to pass on?'

Alex frowned. 'But you're surely going back to Burano today? Let me call him again, he must have missed the point.'

'I don't want to sound ungrateful and I'm sure he was doing his best ... I'd decided I would cut and run ... ' I said, but Alex ignored me, took out his phone and walked to the far end of the room. When he returned, he said, 'I've left him a message. He'll be there when you arrive later today. If not, then call at his house in Mazzorbo. I know him well. He'll want to make amends.' He wrote something down on a notepad and tore the page off, thrusting it towards me. 'Here. Directions. And don't argue. It's done.' He then waved his arms about him. 'How do you like the place, by the way?'

I said, 'It's certainly stunning. My mother would be thrilled. There seem to be rooms leading to other rooms, leading to staircases and balconies ... It's almost a small palace.'

Alex laughed. 'It's not quite a palace, I'm afraid. I'll tell you about it if you've five minutes. It's called Tre Oci – the House with Three Eyes. Mario De Maria, the artist who built this place, was an early Symbolist painter. He helped organise the first Venice Biennale with some friends in 1895. He was also a photographer and an architect known as 'The Divine Painter of the Moon!'. He liked to create evocative images and to depict the most fantastic and unusual aspects of nature.

'The "Eyes" are the three large windows you see in front of you. The house was designed to be a pint-sized, idiosyncratic replica of the Doge's Palace. If you look out of any of the Eyes it's the Doges Palace that stares right back at you across the water. The Eyes have their own story,' he continued. 'You'll like it. His daughter Silvia, the apple of his eye, apparently, died aged nine sometime in the late 1890s leaving him grief-stricken. He went to Paris to recover, took a cure and returned to Venice. He was then living opposite here, in Venice proper, but the memory of Silvia continued to haunt him. So, he decided to build this place as a memorial to her. Tre Oci was finished in 1913.The windows represent his three surviving family members – his wife, his son Astolfo, and himself. People think it's a Renaissance pile but it's a modern pastiche and one of the principal examples of neo-Gothic architecture in Venice. That's it.'

Stella said, 'It seems a shame. One of those windows should be Silvia's.'

'There's a small painting of her in the room where you slept last night. You'll like some of his work. Come here and look.'

There was a laptop on a table nearby. He began flipping through various images: peasant women crossing a bridge at twilight, more women washing clothes in a communal bath in near darkness. Alex paused at a painting depicting medieval-looking figures stripping the clothes from a dead man while in the background through a small door a furnace roared. Human skulls were scattered around the door. 'This one's called "Sinful Souls Resurrected." It's inspired by a legend associated with the slopes of Mount Vesuvius where criminals were once executed and buried. At midday their souls were said to rise up in order to torture and kill unsuspecting travellers.'

Alex laughed. 'His paintings often featured skeletons or monks with no eye-sockets, corpses that come to life – just like in Baudelaire's poems or in Edgar Allan Poe's tales. Do skeletons frighten you, by the way?' he said.

'In ghost trains, yes, real ones? No.'

'Follow me,' he said. They left the studio, climbed some stairs and arrived at the room where Stella had woken earlier that morning. Alex indicted to the picture above the fireplace. 'That's Silvia. Painted by de Maria. I bought the picture from a dealer for almost nothing. The Maria family like the idea that she's still here, Mario's tragic daughter.'

Stella saw again the unsmiling girl in a high-buttoned dress with her hair tied back by a red bow. She had a high forehead, dark arched eyebrows and overlarge eyes. She stared out, lacking any identifiable expression, as if mesmerised. Stella said, 'It's signed by someone called Marius Pictor. That's the second time I've heard that name ... '

'Mario's nom de plume. But I wanted to show you something else.'

He turned around to face the ornate fireplace supported by the two carved female figures. 'You see these two caryatids? Mario added a Gothic touch to the house! What you do is this. Rest your hand on the forehead, midway between the eyebrows, of the figure to your left as you stand opposite to the fireplace, then press the head inwards as if you were pushing it against the wall behind.'

He rested a hand on the forehead of one of the figures and pushed. A sound of jarring iron was audible.

'This sets in motion some hidden machinery that turns the hearthstone on a pivot,' he said. 'Watch,' as the floor in front of the fireplace revolved to disclose a small dark cavity. Looking into the hole, Stella saw what appeared to be a bicycle pedal attached to a small wheel. Alex knelt and began to push the pedal round. He said, pointing, 'Keep your eye on that panel in the corner of the room,' and Stella turned to see a door open in the wall revealing another dark void within. 'There's room enough in there for someone to stand easily at full length. Let's see,' Alex said. He reached into the gloom of the cavity and turned, now cradling something in his arms. It was a small skeleton complete with what appeared to be an oversized skull. It was a shock to her, to be looking at something so strange. Her hangover surged within her and she could say nothing.

Alex bent back down and replaced the remains. 'The method of closing the cavity is equally simple,' he said. 'Turn the pedal, the panel door closes. Press the caryatid's forehead and it slides back out and, with a bit of luck, the hearthstone slides back into position and no one's the wiser. You're just about the only person I've show that to. You can't guess whose remains they are?'

'Surely not Silvia? Was that her skeleton?'

'I found them when I was renovating the building.'

'And you keep them here? Aren't you supposed to report such discoveries?'

'Mario placed her here, that's enough for me.'

'What about the family? Don't they know?'

'Who's going to tell them? Anyway, I don't think of her as a corpse, more an integral part of the house.

'The Tre Oci isn't her monument then, it's her grave,' Stella said.

'I never thought of it like that,' Alex said. 'We've got different temperaments.'

'I must go,' Stella said. 'Thank Franco for rescuing me and thank you for showing me your house – and its secret. It is a secret, isn't it?'

'I don't tell everyone, no. Just people I like.' At the front entrance, Alex said, 'You could come back for dinner this evening. I cook a very nice pasta. '

'I'm early to bed – a flight back home at 8 a.m.'

'That's a shame.'

As she stepped out into a stiff morning breeze, Stella shivered and pulled her jacket about her. Alex said, 'Wait,' and he hurried away, returning with a thick scarf, 'It's my daughter's. She never uses it.' As he placed the scarf around her neck, his small hands brushed the sides of her arms.

7

IT WAS ONLY WHEN I BOARDED the waterbus to travel to Burano that I realised how unwell I felt. A mist was descending upon the whole Lagoon shrouding everything beyond a few hundred yards. Closer at hand, the green plastic covering of the boat's interior reflected the murkier green of the water while the boat's engine sent petrol exhaust bubbling up from beneath the swirling water. Checking my messages, I saw that I had one from Irene saying, 'Stella, if you're still here, can you come and see me at my hotel? I have something I must ask you. You can call at any time, early or late. But please come!'

Irene Foster wanted to speak to me. What could I say to her? That her father was coming here looking for a long-lost, maybe dead, perhaps stepsister of hers? Had they looked into Foster's phone and tracked Keef's message? Would I find myself involved with Keef again and his wild goose chase? Another day entangled in that conundrum wasn't attractive. I pushed the thought to the back of my mind. I had more immediate problems.

There was little to see from the open stern of the waterbus other than a dazzling white wall so I retreated inside, still feeling sick and conflicted. Unless the mist lifted there was no point in setting out for the marshes in a small boat. It was also clear to me that Remigio would have no reason to behave any differently than he had on the previous day.

At the Burano boat station, I waited at the appointed time and place but after fifteen minutes I decided to give up. I had his address on the piece of paper Alex had given me and I felt I ought to pay for the previous day's Lagoon trip, despite Alex's refusal to accept anything on his behalf. I went into the nearest shop where, surrounded by tourist tat – embroidered tablecloths and towels, handkerchiefs, and nightgowns – I asked how I might find Remigio's house.

The girl at the counter said, 'You must walk back to the waterbus station, then bear right and go on till you reach the wooden footbridge. Follow the pathway till you reach the canal, then walk back to the Mazzorbo boat stop.'

Mazzorbo itself was a little island, with stretches of cultivated land dividing scattered housing, much of it small, shack-like bungalows with old boats and discarded furniture littering the back yards. Stella walked along the Mazzorbo quayside, passing drawn-up fishing nets and boats, past tidy little houses, some sporting inflated plastic Santas climbing chimneypots. On the opposite bank stood various tumbledown buildings sporting faded 'For Sale' signs.

Remigio's house was double fronted and painted a deep blue with a small balcony above the front door. There was no bell, so Stella knocked hard on the door. From somewhere deep within the house there came an indistinct call for her to enter so she turned a handle, stepped inside and found herself in a large room dominated by a wooden table that separated a kitchen area from a larger living room beyond. The floor was tiled and spotless; a wood fire burned low.

As she stood waiting, there came a movement beyond accompanied by a shuffling sound. An old woman pushed through a striped curtain which was drawn across the entrance to a staircase. Her thick, silver hair was coiled and she wore a heavy cardigan over a plain blue dress. Her olive features were marked by deep, creased furrows.

I said 'Hullo' and the woman inclined her head, smiled and reached out to me. I realised that the old lady was blind, so I took her hand and was held by a firm grip. The old lady then passed her fingers across my forehead, nose, and lips. Her forefinger then rested on the space between my eyebrows. She said something soft in a dialect I could not understand. She pointed to herself and said, 'Elena,' and then touched my chest with a finger. 'You?'

'Stella,' I said, and in Italian, 'I have come to see Remigio ... '

'You will be cold ... ' she said and ushered me towards the fire.

I stood before the fire while the old lady tossed some wood onto the flames.

She said, 'Remigio will be here soon. Would you like something to eat?'

It was warm and quiet and I felt like sitting and doing nothing. 'Thank you,' I said. She made me coffee and brought some sweet rolls, baked, she said, in her own oven.

'Have you always lived here?' I asked.

'Yes,' she said. She was a 'Buranella', born on the island, she said, in this very kitchen like her mother before her. She told me of her life as a young girl, rising at five in the morning to prepare the stove and the breakfast before beginning to work. She had been a lace-worker, she said, trained at the Burano Lace School. She told me how she had kept house for her mother and how she had moved away to live with her husband, just a few doors away. There was then no running water, she said, so she would take a bucket to the well, and for milk she would go to a neighbour whose little girl would fetch fresh milk from a farm nearby. She laughed at this, as if I might not believe her, turning towards me, and I laughed in return.

Her gentle tones, her hand gestures conspired to send me into a sort of daze. I think I must have momentarily dozed off, for I felt her reach out and touch my face again and take my hand. 'You are unhappy?' she said. I shook my head, realised she couldn't see me and said, 'No, no.'

She then tugged at my hand and I found myself being led further into the house. We reached the back wall of the long room where an arrangement of white patterns hung, softening the darkness.

'Everything here by my hands,' she said. I found myself examining beautiful pieces of handmade lace. Delicate lines of decoration stretched like spiders' trails between garlands of tiny flowers made of thin-gauge thread. The woman asked me if I liked the lace constructions. She then passed her fingers over my cheek to feel my smile.

We climbed a narrow flight of stairs and entered her tiny bedroom. There was a single bed in a corner by a small television broadcasting Mass from the Vatican in soft, soothing tones. Various-sized crucifixes were tacked to the walls. From a small landing one could look out across the canal to the overgrown, deserted island where derelict houses stood, inhabited it seemed only by flocks of birds.

Back downstairs she went to a cabinet and took out a small, framed picture. She handed it to me and I saw, stitched in lace, the face of a man. He had downcast eyes and a thick moustache. At the base of the frame was written, 'Il Pescatore'— 'The Fisherman.' Elena's face was turned towards me all the while, a smile on her lips and I knew who the man was.

'Was this your husband?' I said. She nodded, pleased. 'He is very handsome,' I said.

'Yes,' she said. She took back the picture and stared at it.

An hour had passed. Remigio was clearly not going to arrive. I said to Elena, 'I must go,' and she shrugged and smiled.

As I reached the door, I tried to give her some money. 'For Remigio,' I said. 'I owe him this for a boat trip,' but she shook her head and instead she placed something wrapped in tissue paper into my hands. I took it without thinking, imagining it was one of her delicious rolls, and kissed her on the forehead.

Sitting waiting for the waterbus to return to Venice I opened the package Elena had given me and was shocked to see it was 'The Fisherman'. Why had she given me this precious memento? She didn't know me at all. It was so unexpected that I thought she had made a mistake; perhaps thought I was trying to buy some lace. Too late to go back and too confusing.

Back on the mainland I googled the airline in search of a flight back that evening, but there was nothing available. I had to stay until tomorrow. That left Irene and her request to meet again. It was obvious that she had

seen the phone messages and would want to know who had called her
father. I resolved to tell her about Keef and apologise for my part in the
deception. Keef, wherever he was, would have to sink or swim.

'Stella, you came after all! I told Seth you would but he didn't believe me!'
Irene said as she hugged Stella before sinking back down onto a couch. She
patted the space beside her inviting Stella to join her. Stella saw various
English and Italian newspapers spread across the coffee table open to display
articles and obituaries of Harold Foster. 'Have you seen all this! I had a
good cry last night but this is just making my head spin.' She took a deep
breath. 'You got my message?'

Stella was about to start her apology but Irene raised her hand to silence
her. 'Hear me out,' she said. She was working on Harold's funeral, she
explained. It was going to be quiet and dignified and it was going to be held
in Venice. 'Right here!' she said, laughing.

Various dignitaries and artists had already been invited and she wanted
some of Harold's ashes scattered in the Lagoon by the Biennale Gardens,
no less, the rest to be taken back to England. It would, she said, be a feather
in the cap for Venice. The city hadn't had a celebrity burial for many years.
She was contacting more guests and was busy compiling a list. There would
be a much bigger memorial service and a retrospective exhibition back in
England but for now she wanted a small but 'stunning' event with a
cremation that needed some careful planning. 'And, that's where you come
in. I want you to work for me. Be my Girl Friday. Literally, that's when the
funeral will take place.'

'Friday?' Stella asked.

'Harold was Jewish. Not Orthodox, but no matter. The authorities
here will bend whatever regulations need bending. We already have a
Rabbi. I just need someone to be my Italian voice for an hour or so
during the next couple of days. We need to sort out an itinerary for the
events, get the right people on board. A restaurant, some menus. You run
events, that's what you do, so don't protest! I looked up your track record
in London. Impressive! Greenwich Theatre, The Place, the Hip Dance

Festival, the London Dome thing! You speak perfect Italian. We could work from here. I've set up a desk in the next room where there's a computer already connected.' She moved closer to Stella. 'You were the last friendly face Harold looked into! I like that. It's as though you were meant to happen.'

When Irene sat back, Stella took a deep breath and said, 'But Irene, I'll be on my way to the airport tomorrow morning, on my way home. I'm really flattered, honestly, but –' but again Irene held up her hand.

'We'll get you a nice room here down the corridor so we could consult each morning. This hotel is fabulous. Did you know it was where the Biennale's opening dinner was held, with the President of Italy, the Prime Minister, the mayor of Venice, all here! They're the sorts of people I want at the funeral. I could run names and such past you and then you could liaise with the authorities here, do some of the contacting. You could even continue with some of your ecology work, maybe? Once we get the will settlement sorted, we'll start working with an agent in London who'll handle Harold's work. He's allowed his profile to dip terribly, you know. An artist needs his work to appear regularly, to maintain its value. You'd have a lot to do here, believe me, and we would pay a top salary.'

'I have work to go back to, Irene,' Stella said. ' I only took a couple of days out and I'll be back tomorrow with a contract to fulfil. Even if I wanted to ... ' which she knew was the wrong response and Irene smiled sheepishly. 'I'm ahead of you, sweetheart! I spoke to your boss, Diana Haversham? In London. She was thrilled for you! She'll shift the contracts. I can see by your face that it's a shock. Go and take a walk for five minutes, get some fresh air. You look pale, by the way. You're not ill are you? Go out, have a walk and call Diana but don't say a word till you come back,' and she gently ushered Stella out into the hotel corridor. 'Go, think about it but, don't say no ... '

I stood outside the Hotel Bauer its Art Deco windows now bathed in a luxurious golden light. A group of gondoliers were laughing and larking about by the canal bank, one of them performing a mock-break dance to music playing on a transistor radio while the others clapped hands and blew clouds of cigarette smoke into the afternoon air.

It seemed, on the one hand, that everyone I met here was intent on dragging me to and fro as though I was a small girl. Donato, Keef, then Alex. Remigio had ignored my wishes, his mother had manipulated me in another, mysterious way. Now Irene wanted – had actually taken steps – to take over my life. Yet if I simply ran away, how would that look? I had a sudden desire to take control of the situation. I even experienced a rush of excitement. A celebrity funeral in Venice. A few days, no more. Irene was right. It was 'what I did' and the sooner I got back to doing it the better.

When Stella returned, Irene stared at her for a moment before clapping her hands. 'I can tell you're staying!' she said, and she reached out and embraced Stella once again.' What a relief!' she said, 'and it's strange, I've only known you for a few moments but I feel I've known you for years! It's serendipity!'

Stella said, 'I just hope I can be of use here. There seems such a lot to be done, a funeral in a few days . In Italy?'

Irene waved her hands in front of her. 'Seth will arrange a contract and an account for you and that room.' She looked Stella up and down. 'Is this all you have to wear? You must get something smarter. You'll be meeting people, not wild fowl! There are lovely clothes shops just outside here. We'll fit you out ... '

We spent an hour on the Salita S. Moisè in designer clothes shops enveloped in a warm fug of scented candles, mood music, working our way through rack after rack of expensive clothes. Irene moved here and there swiftly pulling things off shelves, posing me, watching as I donned and discarded a variety of items, murmuring, 'You look fine, that looks so chic!'

Back in Irene's suite I stood in front of a mirror dressed in black pin-striped trousers, a long-sleeved jersey top decorated with sequins and beads, a cardigan and a short blue wool cape. Irene stood behind me and said, 'Now we'll have to find you a nice man to fall in love with. I'll show you your room,' she said and led me to the floor above where we entered a pastel pink bedroom lit by a chandelier and draped in mock Chinese tapestries.

The rest of the afternoon we spent discussing the funeral arrangements. The guest list, the ordering of water taxis to ferry arriving guests from the railway station to suitable hotels, exactly where a post-funeral meal might happen. There was a jungle of red tape to deal with. Compliance with insurance, legal, health and safety obligations and permits for scattering a deceased person's ashes. 'Seth is taking care of those issues,' Irene said. 'He's a lawyer. He says we can't scatter ashes where we want, that we have to take them out into the Atlantic or somewhere, for ecological reasons. I told him, "Screw the ecology. Harold's ashes will be scattered somewhere in the Lagoon, near where the Biennale is held." Wagner's remains were carried that way. Did you know they gave Wagner a funeral of the most theatrical possible proportions? There was a massive flotilla, hundreds of boats, a complete orchestra on barges; people crowded the quays and balconies along the Grand Canal in a show of final respect. That's what Harold should get.'

She then grabbed a glossy brochure from the table and flicked through the pages. She pointed to a blue urn. 'We can have the ashes placed in this, what do you think? Some people throw rose petals or flowers into the water afterwards.' She put an arm round Stella and pulled her close. 'This is a fascinating replica of Roman urns used over a thousand years ago. They're made of sand and gelatine so they dissolve completely in water. They float for a few minutes then submerge. Seth's already ordered one. We just need the permits.'

Irene at last went off to take a nap and as I left her room Seth took my elbow. 'Can we have a word? I was looking at Harold's messages on that little phone of his that you returned to us. There was a hotel number in Venice. I called it and they said someone had cancelled a room. Was that you?'

I said, 'I'm sorry. In fact, Seth, there was something I wanted to tell you ... ' but Seth interrupted me. 'It's okay. The room had to be cancelled.

I rang them, did Irene tell you? They won't tell me anything about who made the booking, only that he was called Pictor but that rings no bells. You see, I have this theory that Harold was coming here hoping to live some of that old bohemian life again, perhaps escape the confinement of his studio. There must have been someone else involved. Maybe this Pictor person would know? Could you go visit the hotel and check? It may come to nothing but if someone was meeting him here, and had arranged the booking, it might tie up some loose ends. Also, I need places to recommend to people coming here for the funeral, not the tourist spots, preferably an old cafe, off the beaten track, style place, the real Venice. Someone suggested this place, the Locanda Montin. Have a look and let me know as soon a you can.' He handed me a piece of paper on which he'd written the two locations. 'Call me if you get anywhere.'

And then I was back outside, breathing in the sharp evening air, a brilliant moon hovering over the Grand Canal.

I found the hotel without difficulty, close by the Accademia. The young woman behind the check-in desk consulted the previous two days' bookings.

'Yes,' she said, 'a Mr Pictor reserved a room for two days but it was cancelled.'

'Had the room been booked in person?' I asked.

'No, over the phone.'

'Not the internet?'

'No, a phone call.'

'Someone in Venice?'

'Maybe,' she shrugged.

'Do you have the number?'

'It's not possible to tell you the number.'

'But you have a record of it?'

'Are you a policewoman?'

'I feel like one,' I said.

It was no use: she was adamant that there was no number and I pushed no harder. I would tell Irene and Seth that whoever booked the room

remained a mystery, which was true, in a way. Where was the Locanda
Montin, I asked. 'Go down to the Zattere, turn right, walk along the front
until you reach Fondamento di Borgo, turn right and follow the canal and
you will find Locanda Montin. Have a nice day!'

The Locanda Montin was identified by a dim lantern above an unremarkable canal-side doorway. Inside, Stella found an almost empty dining room and a bar manned by a single attendant. The walls on both sides of the long room were covered with framed paintings and photos and the room was silent but for the muted conversation emanating from a couple seated close by the door. It looked to Stella nothing like the kind of venue that would appeal to Irene's guests and she prepared to retreat.

As she did so, the barman gestured to her. Simultaneously, she heard a familiar voice at her shoulder. 'What are you doing here?' It was Alex Osbourne.

'I could ask you the same question,' she said.

'I live in this city and this is where I lunch, or used to. You, on the other hand, should be on a plane, winging your way back to London. And what are you wearing? You look like you've aged ten years" he said.

'I've a job,' she said.

The barman was now approaching as they stood in the doorway. Alex nudged her forward, said something to the man and they were ushered to a small, unlaid table.

'You'd like something to drink?' Alex said. 'And what do you mean, a job?'

I told him about Remigio's no-show in Burano, about meeting Remigio's
mother on Mazzorbo, and about travelling back to the mainland intent on
leaving, only to be startled by Irene Foster-Wyatt's sudden offer. At the
sound of her name Alex stared hard at me, genuinely shocked, it appeared.
'Harold Foster's daughter?' he said. 'Foster died on a plane coming here,
the day you arrived. It's all over the news.'

'I didn't explain that part, I'm sorry. Foster and I got on the plane

together,' I said. 'I was the last person to speak to him.' Alex continued to stare; his eyes riveted on my face. 'I can't believe it,' he said.

'Neither can I,' I said.

'You really are an enigma, aren't you?' he said, 'Did you model for Foster?'

'Of course not! I met him at the airport. I helped him with his bags ... '

'And now you're helping with his funeral?'

'I'm helping his daughter with some of the details: hotels for guests, arrangements for the funeral day, transport. If they manage to get it done in such a short time it will be a miracle ... '

'No, no, there's more to it than this!' he said, but just then my phone rang: it was Irene. 'I must answer this,' I said, standing and walking away from the table. 'I'm very sorry. Irene, I'm a bit busy, in company.'

'Just checking, I had a fright,' Irene said. 'They pulled some poor tourist out of a canal and I was afraid something might have happened to you! No one seemed to know where you were.'

'Seth sent me out on a task. I'm fine. I'll see you tomorrow,' I said.

'This is going to be like having a surrogate mother, I can sense it,' I said to Alex as I sat down again. You know this place well?' I said. 'They seem to know you here ... '

He looked about him for a moment as if seeing the place for the first time.

'Too well ... ' He stood and went across to look at a painting of a Venetian square hanging on the wall. 'One of my earliest,' he said. He sat back down, and lowered his voice, 'This was a favourite restaurant of mine in my younger days, but over the last twenty years, I'm sad to say, it's aged badly, it's living on its past reputation. Cover charges, charges for bread, average food, sullen waiters ...

'I remember coming here to Montin's one lunchtime and I ate in the garden. I was alone, surrounded by old-fashioned wooden chairs and benches, yet the atmosphere was so ... it was wonderful. A meal cost a 1,000 lire. There was always a table here for artists. It was a place with a payment plan not unique to these parts, an enlightened view of extended credit. The world was very different then, there were no credit cards but there was credit. Art was legal tender. A lot of these paintings on the walls were extended credit. I was struggling to get established as an artist, couldn't sell anything, only pavement artist stuff. My bill here got so heavy that when, finally, I had an exhibition I told the proprietor to select one piece to cover my bill. When I came by sometime later I said, where is my picture? He said, "You're eating it."

'Talking of eating,' and he waved to the man behind the bar, left some money on the table and beckoned to me to follow him . 'Come on, I'll cook you something. We're just across the water from here, two stops. Don't say no ... '

They caught the waterbus at the Zattere stop. Stella watched reflected lights breaking and dancing on the water's surface as the Giudecca shoreline took shape, emerging from the darkness, its small cafes like illuminated boxes. Above, the western sky was faintly visible. As they neared the stop near the Tre Oci she realised it was the first time she had seen the building from the water. She was entranced by its neat, symmetrical beauty, unlike the tired shabby splendour and faux decadence on display along the Grand Canal. Lit by the streetlamps, she now saw it in all its strangeness. Its oriental diamond patterned brickwork façade was dominated by three enormous shuttered windows which bulged out beneath exaggeratedly peaked arches. Each window possessed a semicircular art nouveau iron balcony with black lace-like balustrades while the central window was crowned by a smaller quatrefoil window construction in the shape of a flower. Its decorative white masonry seemed to glow. Its orange brickwork burned. A zigzag crenelation, like tiny bow-legged men, ran along the top façade, the whole construction dominated by tall inverted Venetian-style chimney stacks.

They alighted and Alex said, 'Quick, we can see the last light, follow me!' and he ushered her through one of the building's main doors, down a corridor and thence to a set of winding stone steps that led up in near darkness to a door in the roof reached via a small wooden ladder.

Alex pushed it open and the dark but glowing night sky was visible. Climbing up behind him, Stella stepped out onto the roof and onto a small, narrow pathway flanked by heavy roof tiles on one side and the zigzig tracery that she had seen from the water forming a knee-high fence on the other. To the right loomed the Santa Croce church, its white dome luminous in the semi-darkness. Away across the water stood the Campanile Tower in St Mark's Square and the Doge's Palace, the latter also shimmering white; the wind whipped flimsy rain against her face.

'This is amazing,' Stella said, 'Absolutely amazing. What a day, what a crazy day!'

8

*BACK DOWNSTAIRS IN THE STUDIO, ALEX took my coat and
threw it onto a cluttered sofa and said, 'Are you hungry? Not a vegan, I
hope. I'm cooking some polenta to go with some prawns. Very Venetian,
though the fish is frozen, I'm afraid. Very bad taste, but it's that time of
year. Fish is my speciality. You fry the prawns in garlic and chilli pepper
and some olive oil, add tomato purée, and breadcrumbs and cook for ten
minutes then serve with the polenta. Sound okay? And wine? What do
you drink with fish?'*

'Dry white?'

*'Exactly.' He disappeared and returned with a bottle. 'Terre Valse
Cococciola. Nice and cold. You sit down and I'll tell you how I came to live
here.'*

*I did as I was told, found a large armchair. Alex took a sip of wine and
gestured around him.*

He said, 'Before you ask, how did I come to live here? Simple story. I was
on the verge of moving away from here on to Florence or Rome when I
heard some people were making a film on the Giudecca, an Italian 'Love
Story' on a shoestring budget, very famous film in Italy now. A couple of
scenes were to be shot here at the Three Eyes and up on the roof where

you've just been. They needed someone to play piano. I used to make a little money playing boogie and blues in cafes so I came over and got the job. It was here I met Toti Dal Monte, a wonderful Italian soprano who had a small part in the film. She lived in an apartment on the Grand Canal and she took a shine to me, I was invited there and met lots of influential people. She was a wonderful person. I drew and painted her, which was my big break, selling drawings and paintings of Toti. It helped establish me in a small way and I earned some real money.

'A group of students lived here as it had been leased to various painters and dreamers for decades. It was crumbling and run-down, the roof was caving in, the foundations were rotting, the ground floor stank from periodic flooding – there was archaic electric wiring all over the place – the whole building, it was a death trap! Each student had a little room. When one of them left to go to Japan he gave me his. Then another lent me this studio. He didn't return either. When they installed gas, the owners needed someone to collect money for the meters ... that was me. When the first bill arrived, the students disappeared! I had the whole place to myself. Sounds so simple doesn't it?

'I negotiated with the de Maria family who still owned the place. Once I'd seen it, I knew I had to live here but buying property in Venice back in the 1980s wasn't easy. And nobody would touch the Giudecca. It was then a kind of low-rent refuge for the broke and bohemian classes. It took years of ingratiating myself with the de Maria estate and its controllers because to sell to someone like me was unusual, to say the least. It was a delicate, tortuous process. It was my devotion to Mario's art that convinced them. He built the place and I saw myself as its guardian. I really believe that. The Three Eyes must always be owned by an artist, like me. The family were impressed by that. They're regretting it now, though.'

'Because it's all yours ... ?' Stella said.

'Mine and various banks and significant others who've lent me money in the past. There are interest payments that are crippling and you wouldn't believe what it costs to maintain this place, it's a colossal expense and rising by the day. The pressure to sell is mounting but I'm resisting. I need a change of fortune, a lucky break. The gallery also costs a fortune but I have to stay there to earn my living. It's a strain, though. People don't spend money like they used to for one reason or another.

'But you're hungry and I've to cook something. Pour another drink and relax. The kitchen's next door and I'll get it started. Did you manage to look at this?' he said and took up the coffee-table catalogue of his work that he'd given to me in his gallery. 'This thing is my latest expense.'

Alone, I turned it over and skimmed the back cover blurb that told of his decades in the city, his remarkable life, how his work celebrated La Serenissima past and present, and how his inventive use of colour was an 'eloquent testimony to his love of is adopted city'.

The images within were familiar to me now and I closed the book and, lulled by the peace and quiet of his studio, closed my eyes. When I opened them, Alex had returned and was holding the catalogue .

'Harold Foster and I are – were – different painters but I think we shared the same concern with form and subject matter, that one of the highest aims in art is to depict human flesh, preferably female, although I sometimes feel that he's not really painting living things. Have you seen any of his pictures? You will have. They look like glimpses of what the subject will be like just after dying, which just seems a bit ghoulish to me. I like to feel my paintings are full of life. Where we differ, big time, is the market. Do you know how much one of his paintings goes for these days?

'I know very little about him,' I said.

'Millions. It's remarkable how much money they fetch. Absolutely staggering. Do you know what one of my full-length portraits costs?'

I shook my head.

'20,000 euros,' and he gave me a resigned-looking smile.

'All the same, I can't imagine he's got a place like this, whatever his paintings sell for,' which sounded crass but I felt uncomfortable talking about painting, his or anyone else's.

'No, no, that's true. And he won't have had as much fun as I've had here.' He waved his hand about him. 'This isn't just a studio, as you can

see. It's a stage. It operates as a background to my paintings. The things scattered about here are props, and people who pose here become characters. I've had rock stars here, writers, musicians, some of Venice's most eminent citizens. Great parties. Great times. Did you get a chance to look at the catalogue? Cost a fortune to have it printed.'

My heart sank but I'd given the problem some swift thought and said, 'I like the Venetian scenes: the markets and the canal views, all the familiar sights. They're like brightly coloured jigsaws with each plane slotting into place like abstracts.'

'I should have got you to write the blurb!' he laughed. 'Anything else?'

'And it's ingenious the way the geometric structure of a building or a bridge or a campanile finds a sort of rhythmic echo in the mooring posts and distant towers.'

'Rhythmic echo. I like that, too.'

I wasn't sure if he was mocking me ...

'But what about the portraits, the posed figures?' he continued.

I began to feel irritated by his insistence, sensing that he really didn't care too much about what I felt. Whether it was the effect of the wine, or a desire not to be seen as too ingratiating, I took a deep breath.

'You're probably going to throw me out now but these semi-clothed girls sitting in front of dressing-room mirrors with their Japanese fans remind me of glamour illustrations. 1950s style. They feel to me like pure titillation.'

'He raised his eyebrows and nodded. He wasn't taking me seriously. I sensed that anything I said just amused him. 'I think you've missed something there,' he said. 'Look, the attraction of the nude is that it isn't titillating. Someone once said that Harold Foster's female subjects (we were back to Foster again) seemed not just nude but obtrusively naked. Foster and I at least have that in common: the attraction of the nude is precisely that it is not titillating. Instead of being nude they become naked.'

I couldn't help laughing. 'That's clever! Naked except for the suspenders and stockings which make the models look like bored, high-end-maintenance mistresses.'

'They might be, for all you know,' he said.

He started again, as if he was giving me a little lecture. 'Take the word model, it's misleading. It implies passivity and objectification, as if the girl's contribution to the picture is on the same level as the folding screen or the bowler hat.'

'Or the suspender belt and stockings?'

'What have you got against suspenders and stockings? Anyway, those are for the husbands and boyfriends!'

'Men actually commission you to paint pictures of their wives like that?'

'Well, maybe not their wives.'

'That's what I mean. Alex, most of these girly paintings have shady motives behind them ... '

'Girly paintings? Shady motives? You think I'm a voyeur? Someone did say that my paintings are a sort of self-portrait,' and he rummaged around for a magazine amid a pile of papers. 'Here, listen, "Osbourne's work teeters on a knife-edge between the ethereal and the erotic. Between nude and naked, between art and pornography.'"

'I didn't say anything about pornography ... '

But he was incorrigible, He was patronising me, but it was like a harmless game and oddly amusing, which was part of his charm, I supposed, because he still possessed that charm, despite his age.

'I try to capture images,' he was saying, 'to hold them in a moment in time. Like the transience of light passing: one moment the image is there, the next it's gone for ever, never the same again ... '

'Now you're trying to baffle me with painterly science,' I said, 'and these paintings are not erotic, believe me ... ', but he'd hurried away to his kitchen and the polenta.

I got up and walked around the studio, the wine now starting to make me feel light-headed and I was afraid I was on the brink of having an argument, despite his indifference to my views. I had a sudden moment of inspiration and when he returned I'd found my rucksack and taken out the lace fisherman that Elena had given me.

'This is the sort of art I feel at home with,' I said. 'It's unpretentious and I can appreciate it without knowing anything about how it's made or why.

It's just itself.' I handed it to Alex who glanced at it before handing it back to me.

'It's nice,' he said. 'Did you buy it? Must have been expensive.'

'Elena gave it to me.'

'Elena? Remigio's mother?'

'I went to their house when I couldn't find him. She was very nice and welcoming.' Alex stared at me without speaking for a moment and I felt awkward, as though I'd overstepped the mark in some way. 'I didn't mean that the lacework was better than your work, just easier for me to appreciate. It's ... '

'Primitive?'

'Not at all! It must have taken so much skill to make it. I wish I'd offered her something for it but I was on the boat before I realised what it was that she had given me,' I said.

'That's the point. You can't buy this stuff any more. Most of what's on sale is made in China. Same goes for Murano glass. It's economics. There aren't enough people around who appreciate the craft sufficiently to pay for the labour involved.

'So how long do you take to finish a painting? There seem to be three or four on the go here.'

'Small portraits, that's head and shoulders only, can generally be completed in two or three sittings, usually one morning and one afternoon. Larger figure compositions, that's three-quarters or full-length, may take up to five sittings. A long weekend is often enough. Or I work from photos. Why, are you thinking of having your portrait done?'

'Do you think Harold Foster's paintings took as long as that?' I said, and immediately regretted it, but Alex just said, 'Supper is served!'

We sat at a small table he'd set up in the studio. He opened another bottle of wine.

'To answer your point, or the one I think you were making, his approach isn't comparable to mine. People of all kinds come here to be painted: academics, politicians, entertainers. But they pay me. No one pays Foster. And most of my commissions are from women. They want to explore their fantasies. That's what my paintings try to do. In one particular painting, a

84

very nice commission, the woman is wearing a black dress,' and he pointed across to where a dress was hanging. He laughed softly to himself. 'You'd be amazed how often that dress has come in useful! It's those theatrical fantasies associated with the depravities of Weimar cabaret. So many women want to be Sally Bowles! I've been doing cabaret and theatre pieces for decades. I once built a real stage in the studio and we had theatre lighting and costumes and we put on a full production of Cabaret. But time moves on. In fact, I've been working on something more appropriate to the Three Eyes. You've heard of Salome?'

Before I could say yes, he continued,

'Of course, you have. The stepdaughter of King Herod. She calls for the head of St John the Baptist after he rejects her sexual advances. Herod at first refuses but gives way when she says she'll perform the Dance of the Seven Veils because he secretly lusts after her. She dances and then demands John's head. It's brought in on a platter. When she kisses John's lips and drinks his blood, Herod is so disgusted he has Salome executed.

'Artists have always been fascinated by Salome, depicting her in frescoes, mosaics, engravings, oils. Lots of Mario de Maria's close associates painted portraits of her, people like Von Stuck, Klimt, Gustave Moreau, and Chini, Beardsley and Dalí. Mario even did one himself ... not to mention Titian and Caravaggio, the list is endless. Now then,' he said. 'Come and bring your drink back into the studio, I want to show you something.'

'The polenta was brilliant,' I said. 'Really tasty ... ' but he was busy opening drawers in a cupboard close by.

'Look here,' he said producing a small box containing a pair of ornate, cheap gilt earrings. 'They were made for Rita Hayworth when she played Salome in the Hollywood film version. I bought the earrings in an auction. Put them on!'

'I don't wear earrings,' Stella said. 'No piercings.'
'They're clips.'
She stood before a long mirror and adjusted them, turning her head from side to side as the earrings glittered like tiny spots of gold.

Alex stood behind her. 'They came with documents guaranteeing their provenance. They were originally given as a competition prize by a picture magazine. Here,' and he handed her a copy of a film magazine in a cellophane wrapper dated 5th September 1953 . On the cover was a publicity shot of Stewart Granger and Rita Hayworth.

'Rita Hayworth also wore this,' Alex said, producing a large diamond ring. 'It cost me over $150 a few years ago. See if it fits.'

She held it up to the light. 'I don't want to disappoint you, Alex, but I don't think it's a real diamond.'

'Of course, it isn't. Wait here.' Alex left the room returning moments later holding a long dress on a hanger. It was a Grecian-style floor-length gown of pale blue silk with a sweeping train in the back. At the front, ornate breastplates cut from thin brass sheeting with an inbuilt sewn-in brassiere covered a sheer silk underslip with a matching belt around the waist.

'This,' he said, staring at her unsmiling, 'is Hayworth's "Princess Salome" dress. It was part of the collection auctioned off some years ago. Cost me over $4,000'

'You bought this thing? Can I ask you a personal question?' Stella said, 'Are you gay, by any chance?'

'Very funny. Try it on ... go on. If Irene Foster can doll you up then so can I ... ' and he gestured to a screen in the corner of the room.

'I'm not putting this on ... !' she laughed. 'Really. I never liked fancy dress, even as a child.'

'It'll take a second. Come on, you've done the ring and the earrings ... '

'I think I can see where this is heading,' Stella said as she stepped behind the screen. When she emerged, Alex said, 'I knew it. Perfect fit.' He then dragged a divan away from the wall. 'Lie down here,' he said.

Stella said, 'I was only joking about you being gay! There's no need to make a statement! Is this the casting couch you use for your models?'

'Another difference between Foster and me is that women like the way I treat them, as models, I mean. I don't think he was as well-behaved, but then you may know all about that by now ... '

'You were well-behaved?'

She thought of the pictures on the clipboard of Alex when a young man, tousled and cheeky and looking as if he was having the time of his life with young, gullible girls.

'I'm not going to lie on the couch ... ' she said.

Alex sat on it himself and was silent for a moment. 'Okay, it's like this. I want to produce a painting of Salome. Something I can put in the gallery so that women will say, "I'd like to be painted just like her." The Rita Hayworth touch makes it even more attractive as a selling point. It's a change of direction but in the Mario de Maria spirit. But I need the right model. Professionals are a pain, the infrequency of getting them, the way they waste time, a cigarette here, an extra cup of tea there. The girl I'd hoped to use turned out to be useless. I need someone fresh and striking and, *amateur*. In short, I need *you*.'

'That,' Stella said, 'has to be an absolute joke.'

'You wouldn't be naked,' he said. 'You'll be in Rita Hayworth's dress. You're perfect.'

She laughed again. 'All this lovely polenta and sparkling wine and you were simply lining me up to be a model!'

'It happened suddenly. You see someone and it makes sense. When you appeared in the square the other day, I thought, that's my Salome. Then you reappeared at Montin's. It's – what's the word? – to do with coincidence. Predestination?'

'Kismet?'

He smiled. 'Well, you've certainly got the baubles and the bangles ... ' and he began to sing, "bright shiny beads, tra lala."'

'I won't do it. Apart from the fact that I don't have the time.'

'I think you owe me. I've rescued you from drowning in a canal. I've given you a bed for the night. I've taken you on a tour of my lovely house. I've introduced you to Mario de Maria and Toti dal Monte, wined you in Montin's restaurant and now you're wearing Rita Hayworth's dress. You can have a copy of the picture when it's finished, what more can I say? Women pay hundreds of euros for the privilege. I can promise you that you will not be seduced. Trust me, I'm an artist.'

'You said you work from photos. Why don't you just take photos of me? Last chance, as I won't be dressed like this again, take my word.'

'That's you last word? Okay. I 'll take some for reference. You might change your mind.'

I lay down as Alex indicated, resting my head on the velvet cushions. With deft touches and instructions, he manoeuvred me into a particular position before handing me a fan of purple ostrich feathers.

'Waft it about,' he said, while setting up a camera on a tripod. He took several photos in quick succession. 'Now the head. Stand by the window, 'and he handed me a tray on which he'd placed the head of a tailor's dummy. He'd painted it in garish colours, blood red smears on the neck where the head had been sliced off and he'd stuck a kind of long wig on it.

'That's John the Baptist's severed head. You must stare at him as if you're delighted.'

I could only just manage to keep a straight face. 'I thought she was handed the head after she'd danced the Seven Veils,' I said.

'Too much movement. I've thought about it, though. It's the model question again. Belly dancers are hard to come by.'

'The Dance of the Seven Veils isn't a belly dance.'

'You know about these things, I presume?'

'I did a course in Eastern dance. We get a lot of corporate requests for such things. The seven veils is really just a fanciful westernised version of a Middle Eastern religious observance. During biblical ceremonies women did a sort of chuwl, a Hebrew word which means to twist or whirl in a circular or spiral manner. It was an erotic dance for which they wore a small piece of cloth around the hips, and nothing else. That's where the striptease idea comes from. Whirling is more authentic than belly dancing. I danced it in Turkey on holiday.'

'Give us a whirl, then,' he said.

'In this silly dress?'

'You can take your clothes off if you like. Anyway, you can turn around in that. If you won't model, then whirl.'

I was about to refuse again but it seemed churlish to keep saying no.

'There's got to be music. Dancers spin to the sound of flutes.'

'OK. I'll play piano. Pretend it's a flute.'

He was soon clearing away books and papers from the upright piano in the far corner of the studio. I put the dummy head down at my feet and waited.

'Well, it starts like this. The dancer slaps the floor with his hands, so! That's meant to shock the inner consciousness awake to begin, first walking, then whirling on what's called the bridge Sirat. That's the bridge mentioned in the Koran that must be crossed from this world to reach Paradise on the day of the Last Judgment. I read somewhere that it's as thin as a strand of vermicelli and as sharp as a sabre-toothed tiger tooth.'

'Try saying that with a pebble in your mouth,' Alex laughed, then yelled 'Dance!' and started pounding down on the piano keys.

I took a step forward. As I began to turn in a circle, I said, 'You always pivot on the left foot, pushing with the right foot in a smooth counter-clockwise rotation. In the classical whirling posture, both arms are raised, with the right palm facing up, while the left palm faces towards the ground. Divine energy is believed to cycle through the right palm, heart, and exit out of the left palm into the physical universe ... There's a real stillness you discover at the centre of the whirling ... everyone disappears and you feel as if you're in the eye of a hurricane. You focus your whole being intensely on the divine so that the soul is both destroyed and resurrected.'

I moved faster and faster as Alex began to sing,

'Sadie Cohen left her happy home
To become an actress lady
On the stage she soon became the rage
As the only real Salomy baby.
Don't do that dance, I tell you Sadie
That's not a bus'ness for a lady!'

As I turned and turned, I saw myself, as if from far above, dressed in

89

a garish Hollywood outfit, spinning round in a Venetian palazzo with the Giudecca Canal flowing by outside, a Bohemian artist pounding out a slow blues number on the piano, and I thought, this is some sort of experience ...

Later that night, however, I wondered whether I was becoming something of a jinx. Old men fell over whenever they came near me. Alex had said, 'Look, let me put on a record of piano music and I'll have a go,' and he'd joined me, standing beside me in his stockinged feet. He'd taken up the posture, had stood watching me as I'd pivoted, round and round, before launching himself into a lumbering circle, his hands above his head, his face a picture of sweaty concentration. Which had only caused me to laugh, to double up, in fact, while he'd continued to propel himself round and round until, inevitably, he'd veered away, still twirling, to collide first with the piano stool and finally, to collapse onto a small knee-high drawing bench which had shattered beneath him. Unable to stop laughing I'd fallen onto my knees, tears running down my cheeks until I realised that Alex had hurt himself and couldn't get up. He had strained an ankle and badly bruised his left knee. I'd had to help him up to his bedroom where I'd left him complaining, 'I'll look more like fucking Quasimodo than Herod tomorrow.'

By then it was too late to catch a vaporetto back to the Bauer. I was tired and much drunker than I'd imagined, something of a recurring Venetian theme. What's more, if I was honest I'll admit that I was more than happy to make my way back up to the little room where I'd slept the night before. Somehow the thought of the gaudy luxury of the Bauer Hotel filled me with dread.

I slipped out of Rita Hayworth's silk dress, removed the golden earrings, turned the lock in the bedroom door and I fell asleep once more to the soothing sound of soft rain falling on the skylight window high above me ...

9

IN THE HARSH BRIGHT MORNING LIGHT streaming down from the skylight Silvia de Maria's portrait appeared to Stella to be cracked, peeling and charmless. Beyond her, behind the wall, her desiccated body was locked away, the two female caryatids standing impassively either side of the fireplace.

Stella showered and found Alex sitting in the kitchen looking as if the night before had never happened.

'Did you sleep well?' he said.

'Fine. Did you damage anything?' she said.

'Just an ankle sprain. I was lucky. I could have torn a hamstring,' he said. 'Where to now?'

'Sourcing a restaurant for the funeral guests, I think. Shouldn't be too difficult in this town.'

'Could be disastrous. Let me know where you intend to book. I may know someone who can help out.'

'That's nice of you.'

'Although my last recommendation wasn't too successful, was it? Remigio let me down. Can't think what got into him. Coffee?'

'I must run. It was great fun last night. I'm sorry I can't be Salome. Here's the dress and earrings,' she said, placing the box on a chair. 'Oh, and John the Baptist's head!'

Outside in the fresh morning air she hurried to the waterbus stop just as a boat pulled away. With ten minutes to spare before the next waterbus, she walked on to a small news-stand and gazed at the newspaper headlines. A familiar name caught her eye. She pulled out a copy of *Il Gazzettino* from the rack and saw a picture of a much younger, much hairier, Keef Cottesloe above a headline: LA FAMOSA ROCK STAR ANNEGA IN UN INCIDENTE TRAGICO ...

It felt as though my mind had suddenly emptied of everything else. All went blank so that I was unable to move forward or speak or even respond. I read on:

'Police officer Alessandro Giuliano said divers found the corpse in a canal beneath the Liberty bridge. Fire-fighters recovered his body on Wednesday morning and he was identified by documents on his body. An autopsy has been scheduled to determine the cause of death. Giuliano said there were no indications that the death had been violent but "we are not ruling anything out, any hypothesis". Cottesloe's next of kin have been informed.'

There followed quotes from various fans, rock stars, and a paragraph about the group. Ozzy Osbourne said: 'Keef was a giant! A rock god ... '

I could only turn and hurry back to the House, banging on the door until Alex opened.

'Can we speak?' Stella managed, and wandered into the studio where the remains of last night's wood fire smouldered. Alex followed and stood watching her. 'I'm sorry, I've just had a nasty shock. Where do I start? That tourist Irene mentioned last night, on the phone, the one who drowned? It's in the newspaper.' She handed Alex *Il Gazzettino*.

'Moonstone. I saw them once, supporting Deep Purple. Long before your time,' Alex was saying.

'I know Keef Cottesloe, the man in the paper who's just died.'

'You know Cottesloe?'

'I met him soon after I arrived here. He said he was waiting for Harold

Foster. I told you I got on the plane with Foster. By chance I ended up with his phone and I answered Cottesloe's call. I wanted him to go to the police and meet Foster's relatives when they arrived but there was some mystery about Foster coming here and Keef persuaded me not to say anything to anyone. He had a plan of some sort. I can't go into all the details but I agreed, although it's made life extremely difficult. And now he's dead. I've got to go to the police, haven't I? I was talking to him the other evening when I got drunk and ended up here. I told Irene I had no idea why Harold was coming here. How can I explain all this to her? '

Alex said, 'I'm not really following much of this.'

'I was supposed to meet Keef after meeting up with Foster's relatives. Keef said he'd managed to contact a woman here, an illegitimate daughter of Harold's who was thought to have died here. He'd written songs about the daughter. He said he'd found her here, alive. It was all to do with Keef writing his life-story. I'm not making much sense but it's a convoluted tale.'

Alex sat down in a chair by the door. 'So what are you planning to do?' he said quietly.

'I'm working for Irene so I think I should tell her about Cottesloe. And the police, too. I'm a witness. Again!'

Alex said, 'If I were you, I'd keep quiet, I just wouldn't get involved, particularly not with the Italian police. You'll be roped into all sorts of strange business. Anyway, it sounds hare brained. A *daughter* of Harold Foster's? He must have scores of them, here and there, from what one reads. Sometimes people like Cottesloe get strange ideas into their heads where celebrities are concerned. They think they know them, they write letters to them, claim to be married to them ... '

'Keef had known Harold Foster for a while. He had his phone number.'

'You say you met Cottesloe once? Twice? He died when? A day or so ago? What could you tell the police? He'll be identified by someone and that will be the end of it.'

'I feel like I'm a jinx. People seem to be dying all around me.'

'It's very unfortunate. Apparently he was full of alcohol. Accidents like this happen here occasionally, with water at every turn. It might have happened to you the other night if Franco hadn't stepped in. What can you add? They know who he is. It was an accident. If someone's knocked down by a car or falls under a train, would you go to the police just because you met him a few days previously?'

'I'm working for Foster's daughter. I know important things that she doesn't.'

'Think it through. Would she want to know about Keef's crazy claims? She's burying her father. Can you imagine the complications, linking him with a dead rock star and claims of an illegitimate daughter! All of it is contentious, to put it mildly.'

'They might find some reference to me in Keef's personal effects.'

'Did he have a phone?'

She shook her head. 'He always used pay-phones. He said he couldn't afford anything else. He was broke, lived in a camper van'

'Where's the camper van?'

'I couldn't say, somewhere on the road to the airport.'

'They'll not find it for months. My advice is – don't tell anyone. You owe no one a thing. No one will thank you. If you're worried about people asking you questions, where you were when he died, you can say you were here, which you were. If you need a bolt-hole, then come back here. Stay as long as you like.'

'That's very nice of you. I'm sorry I couldn't model.'

'I never do anyone a favour without calculating what I can get in return. Time is short, by the way. Don't you need to be somewhere?'

As she entered Irene's hotel suite, Stella found herself in the middle of a confusing clamour of people coming and going, mobile phones ringing non-stop. Everywhere there were bunches of flowers in baskets and buckets. Irene embraced her. 'It's wet and wild outside. I hope the rain holds for tomorrow. You didn't use your room last night.'

'I got caught in the bad weather and stayed with a friend on the Giudecca. The hotel couldn't help with that phone call, by the way. The mysterious

Mr Pictor.' She followed Irene through into her bedroom where they sat on the bed and Irene handed her a typed list of names.

'Those are the names of whom we'll be taking on the launches. When the service is over – estimated time 1.30 – the launches will be waiting by the bridge. You need to contact – 'and Irene indicated various names on the list – 'and chat them through it, okay? Provide them with anything they need. Then the launches ferry everyone to Torcello to Locanda Cipriani's where Seth has booked a luncheon. I think it'll be perfect. It has class and history. Did you know it was Ernest Hemingway's favourite haunt? It's dripping with artistic significance. Max Ernst left a drawing there. Chagall, Man Ray, Dufy, Henry Moore, even Bob Rauschenberg – the list goes on! They had Charles and Di for lunch! Can you imagine!'

'Once you've sorted the guest list out, get across to Torcello asap and call me when you get there and tell me what you think about the restaurant. I need to know that it's going to work okay. Seth's only spoken over the phone. I don't want to get there and find it's a disaster. I'd have done it myself but there are so many people to see, I can't get out of this room! You must make some special seating requests, that's very important – here's the list. We just have to make sure it will work. Call me when it's set. I'll want to talk to the proprietor, they're wonderful people but I need to be sure. You understand? Are you okay? You haven't said a word. Were you drinking last night?'

I was glad of the confusion, the sense of disorder all around. It obliterated the need to talk and think about Keef. Once again I sat on the boat heading across the Lagoon towards Burano. My phone rang. It was Alex. I told him I was fine and where I was heading. He knew the restaurant owner. 'I'll give him a call. It might help.'

The journey passed quickly, probably because I was in a trance. I wondered if I would see Remigio on the Burano quay-side but it was deserted. I then took the regular motor-launch that ferried passengers across the short stretch of water to Torcello, a flat strip of land opposite Burano

95

dominated by a 1,000-year-old church tower and where the Cipriani restaurant was situated.

On arrival on Torcello I stood alone on the landing stage watching the boat leave for the return trip to Burano carrying a small group of tourists. I felt the weight of silence pressing down upon me. I then set out along the red-brick zigzig-patterned pathway running beside the main canal that led to the centre of the island.

At a bend in the canal I came across a solitary busker playing what sounded like Viennese waltzes on an accordion. The sound followed me like a lament. I reached a small stone bridge across which, a short way along the farther bank, stood the Locanda Cipriani restaurant. It had a red-tiled roof and wooden balconies. Inside were timbered ceilings with Venetian bas-reliefs covering the walls. Near the bar was a large rustic-style fireplace with a crackling wood fire.

The owner introduced himself. Preparations were all 'in progress', he assured me. The 'maître pâtissier' was creating an assortment of sweet snacks; the sommelier had selected a range of Italian wines to accompany the food and the chef was ready to serve dishes 'created by the Cipriani family'. There would be fish, vegetables, homemade pasta and rice. He took my list of questions and showed me the long table already laid out in the veranda-room with views out onto winter-stripped trees and gardens. He listened as I outlined who was to be where and why. After he'd hurried off, I sat by the fire and called Irene, and described the meal. She said, 'Sounds great. I'll call you back in twenty-minutes with some last-minute updates.'

Stella left the restaurant and walked the short distance to where the ancient cathedral, the Basilica of Santa Maria Assunta, stood looking down on the square that formed the centre of the island. Opposite the cathedral was a small museum, while all around weather-pitted statues, stone monuments and urns had been placed, some mildewed and green, others clean and white. There came the distant clatter of unseen workmen toiling high on scaffolding that enveloped the main cathedral tower. The whine of drills and the occasional voice echoed down to where she stood. Just then the church bells started to toll, only ceasing as the clanging sounds drifted away. The silence seemed to 'sing' long after the bells had finished.

A little white dog hurried past followed by a small, middle-aged woman who went to open up one of the souvenir-stands which was wrapped in tarpaulin. Stella watched as the woman swiftly created a miniature gift emporium. Silk scarves, carnival masks and gondoliers' straw hats were hung in profusion. Stella checked her phone, then looked up and caught the woman's eye. There was a flash of recognition. The two women stared across the square at one another as if transfixed. Stella rose and walked across to her, saying in Italian, 'Hello, remember me?' The woman stared back as if not understanding her.

'We spoke briefly the other morning when you found me in Alex's house on the Giudecca, after I'd disgraced myself. I'd been drunk. You were standing at the bottom of the bed.'

The woman said, almost inaudibly, 'Yes, perhaps.'

'I'm sorting out someone's funeral meal at Cipriani's.'

'A funeral?' the women said in English.

'Yes, a famous artist has died. My name's Stella. You're Maria Pasolini, I know,' and she proffered a hand. 'But you're not Italian, then?'

The woman said, 'I'm Alice Casteret,' taking hold of Stella's hand as if fearing the worst.

At that moment, two Asian tourists appeared, laughing and chattering, making for the stand. They started to examine the souvenirs, picking up masks and trying them on.

'Alice *Casteret*?' Stella asked.

The tourists bought a mask apiece. The woman fumbled with their change, glancing at Stella as she did so. The tourists then stood back taking photos of the souvenir stand.

Stella said, 'Did someone called Keef come to see you recently asking questions?'

The woman stared at her in silence for a moment then said, 'Keef?' and shrugged. Stella pressed on, her heart now thumping hard. 'His name was Keef Cottesloe, he was a large man, about sixty-ish?'

The woman made no reply but took out a mobile phone, turned away and called someone, speaking quietly in Italian before saying, 'I am closing now. My son is coming. Speak to him, please.'

'I seem to have upset you. I'm sorry. You know Alex, though, don't you? But I'm a bit confused – he said you were called Maria, that you were his cleaner.'

The woman began to pull down the gifts strung above her on wires.

Stella said. 'You're not packing up because of me, are you? I don't need to speak to your son. I'm just curious. It seems odd that –'

The woman looked up over Stella's shoulder, the expression on her face causing Stella to turn around. She found herself staring at Franco. He gave a puzzled smile, craning to look round Stella at Alice as if for explanation. Alice said to Stella, 'This is my son. He will talk to you.'

I apologised to the woman and hurried away, perplexed and annoyed. I could make no sense of any of it. I saw on my phone that Irene had called with more messages, more funeral queries, yet another table placement. There was even a message from Alex asking if all was okay at the restaurant. I entered the Cipriani, found the owner, relayed the information to him before hurrying off. The accordion-player smiled up at me as I passed him and I threw down some spare euros. As I waited at the waterbus stage for the motor launch back to Burano, Franco appeared on the pathway. He approached, still smiling.

'I'm sorry. You are upset about something,' he said.

'It doesn't concern you,' Stella said. 'It's okay. I'm sorry if I startled your mother.'

They stood side by side as the launch approached. Franco touched her on the arm and said, 'You don't want to get on this thing. I've a boat moored a little way down from here. Come with me, we can talk about this. There are some things I can tell you that might help explain matters. Come, please,' and he walked away. She watched him go as the launch pulled in. She saw the blank faces of the arriving tourists. It was starting to drizzle. She turned and followed Franco.

Further along the short waterfront she saw he had a small, neat and tidy launch complete with fishing tackle and a small cabin. He reached out and handed her down. She sat inside the cabin as he stood at the stern, tiller in hand. The water swirled away behind as they sped out into the sheen of cold grey water, the tiny engine buzzing like a wasp.

As they moved away from Torcello they entered a marshy environment of mudflats and sandbanks, fields of salt morass raised here and there into shapeless mounds and intercepted by narrow rivulets. As far as the eye could reach, it was a waste of wild sea moor, ashen grey, lifeless, the colour of sackcloth, with the corrupted seawater soaking through the roots of its acrid weeds and gleaming hither and thither through its snaky channels.

She could see the horizon away to the north-east; but to the north and west there was a blue line of higher land, and above this, but further back, a misty band of mountains touched with snow.

'You don't remember this boat, do you?' Franco said, smiling.

'I'm afraid not. I have to thank you, though. Apparently, I could have ended up ... ' and she thought of Keef and couldn't finish the sentence.

'You've been out here before?' he said, 'With Remigio. Didn't it go well?'

'He refused to take me to where I wanted, where I could take any relevant pictures.'

'Pictures for?'

'I'm studying, or rather I was studying, the effects modern-day living is having on the wetlands. They're being eroded by waves made by boats, probably like this one They could be gone in a few years. The salt marshes can't regenerate naturally. I was hoping to take photos to document that. My MA ... '

'Have you got your camera with you?' Franco said. 'I'll give you a tour. I work as a guide sometimes. You want a commentary? It's free!'

For an hour they wove in and out of narrow channels, close to banks and ridges while Stella took photos and made notes. She watched the light changing, the sun slowly dissolving in a dark swirl of ginger tinged with blood.

As they passed a coastline along which ran a long, low wall, Franco said, 'That's the island of Sant'Ariano. Originally it was a monastery, but then it became an ossuary for human bones from Venice during the 16th century when the plague struck. There were so many that passers-by could see them piled high in mounds, so in 1665 it was decided to build a wall along the shores of the island to hide them from view. Until a few years ago, enormous piles of bones barely covered with earth and brambles were still visible. They now are being flattened and access is closed; it's supposed to be haunted. Today, it's disused and said to be plagued with snakes. But that's all for tourists. Haunted islands, ghosts, blablabla. When the tourists have had their trips and indulged in the romance and the scary stories, people still have to live and work here. Talking of which ... '

They had entered a waterway, a small inlet, where Franco cut out the engine. They glided towards a small, shack-like building perched on stilts resting on the bank of the waterway. A voluminous V-shaped fishing net supported by four tall metal pylons straddled the waterway and dwarfed the shack.

'Home from home,' Franco said.

'This is yours?' Stella said.

'Yes, it's a bilancia, a traditional fishing hut.'

Inside the hut, reached by climbing a sturdy little ladder from the landing stage, a long oilcloth-covered table ran along one wall, and opposite stood a stove and sink. A bunk filled space at one end. Maps of the Lagoon and illustrated posters of fish and birds adorned the shellacked-wood walls. In one corner sat an ancient motor.

Franco said, 'Watch,' and he flipped a winch switch to start it up. 'Out there,' he directed, and she saw the large funnel-shaped net slowly descend into the water. 'When it rises and if the catch looks worth it, I paddle my little coracle beneath the net canopy, open the funnel and collect my dinner: soft-shelled crab, whitebait, tiny shrimp, sole, sea bass, eel. Seafood doesn't get fresher – or tastier!'

She looked out across the marshes. The many narrow waterways were like the veins on the back of an old man's hands, forking and meandering away into the gloom. She sat at the table and Franco began to boil a can of water. He said, 'I bought this bilancia four years ago from an elderly man from Burano. I added the motorised fishing net and an outdoor deck. I come out here to fish. I used to shoot ducks from a hide not far from here, but they banned it. I still have the guns ... Alex comes out here, too; he helped pay for it. Not that he's a fisherman. He likes the view, sketches here sometimes. Which brings us back to where we were half an hour ago, I think. You were upset. It must have something to do with Alex.'

'I saw your mother the other morning when I woke up in your father's house after you rescued me. Alex told me that she was his *cleaner* called Maria Pasolini.'

Franco laughed.

'I don't think it's funny. Then there was his wife in Perugia and his daughter.'

'I have a sister?'

'But you *are* his son?'

He laughed. 'Yes, I'm his son.

'So, Alice is Alex's wife?

'Partner. Ex.'

'Are you called Casteret or Osbourne?'

'Casteret.'

'And his wife in Perugia?'

'Not sure about that one.'

'His gallery partner Rebecca?'

'She exists. But why does it matter?'

'When I told Alex, I knew Keef Cottesloe, the man who has just drowned in a canal here, he behaved as if he knew nothing about him when I'm sure he must. Your mother will have told him about Keef, surely?'

'What do you know about Keef and my mother?'

'Keef was searching for a woman called Alice Casteret in Venice. He told me he'd found her. Your mother must be one and the same. There can't be too many Alice Casterets around. Why did she call you so suddenly when I turned up? It was about Keef, wasn't it?'

'Keef claimed she was his ex-girlfriend.'

'So, you know about it? Of course, you would, she's your mother.'

'Keef told me about it.'

'Keef? You've met him?'

'I have to make a confession. The night he drowned, I was trying to tell him he was wrong about my mother. He came to Burano a couple of weeks ago to confront her but she couldn't persuade him he was wrong. So, she told Alex. And Alex told me. I said to Keef that he was wrong about my mother and he was causing her a great deal of stress and worry.'

'He had a picture of her.'

'She said it wasn't her. It was apparently taken thirty years ago. I didn't see it. I didn't meet him to discuss the whys and wherefores. My mother said she wasn't who he claimed she was and that was it.'

'Why all this bother? If he was wrong, it's a simple business to prove it, surely? Why was she so afraid?'

'Keef might've published his story anyway and she'd have become embroiled in a publicity stunt. She's a very private person, she probably only knows half a dozen people in Venice. She told Alex and Alex said to me, "Take some money and buy him off. He wants money." So, I did. The last I saw of Keef Cottesloe he was heading off for Piazzale Roma. He must have got very drunk and fallen into a canal. He was crazy man. Crazy, but nice.'

'You gave Keef money? And he went away? It doesn't sound likely. It wasn't really *about* money where he was concerned.'

'He wasn't happy but what else could he do?'

'It just seems so over the top. If someone comes along and says, "You are X who lived here at such and such a time, I know you, don't you remember me?" and if he's wrong you say, "No, you've mistaken me for someone else." If he says, "I knew your mother, Vivienne," then you simply come out with the details of your real parents.'

'Alice hasn't any.'

'No parents?'

'I've never met any of her family, only an aunt, a sister perhaps, when I was very young. The only relatives I have are on my father's side.'

'Don't you think that odd?'

'She had a strange childhood. She says she never knew her parents. She drifted into Venice on a sort of hippy trail.'

'Then all this might well be true! Keef was filling in the missing pieces! Isn't that a possibility?'

'She says she's not the woman he is seeking. She knows that. I believe her. Alex believes her ... '

'But by denying everything point blank, by giving Keef no evidence to refute his claims, she's encouraging him to think she's hiding something. Then you give him money and that excites him even more because he thinks *you're* hiding something.'

'He took the money and said he was leaving.'

'Are you going to the police now that he's died?'

'That would defeat the original purpose – of protecting my mother.'

'But what a risk! What if someone saw you with him?'

'If they do ask me what I was doing with him, I'll just say I recognised him as a rock star and bought him a drink. I haven't broken any law. If I go to the police and tell them about the money, then they will come and start questioning my mother. They might think that, maybe, I pushed him into the canal. Anything's possible.'

'But why did Alex pretend to me that he knew nothing about Keef, not to mention lying to me about who Alice, your mother, really was. Why didn't Alex tell me he knew all about this business this morning when I was asking whether I should go to the police?'

'He didn't want you to go to the police. He's not really sure about you.'

'Me?'

'You're a bit of a mystery. Another confession. I was at the airport when Foster arrived, or when he was supposed to arrive. When news came that he'd died, there was a lot of confusion. Someone said a woman was involved and was being questioned. That was you. I called Alex and he wondered what you were doing with Harold Foster on the plane, whether you were attached to him, helping him. He told me to follow you out and thence onto the hospital. From the hospital to Keef and then to your hotel. He wondered what you were doing talking to Keef.'

'Why didn't he just ask me? Why all the cloak and dagger business? And why would you do all this?'

'Alex can explain, I simply did what I was asked. I didn't like the idea of stalking you but I thought it was for my mother's sake.'

'What has Foster got to do with your mother?

'Nothing as far as I know. The Foster connection was something else. Something to do with art business ... You'll have to ask Alex.'

'So, meeting Alex on my first day here wasn't by chance?'

'Not at all. I followed you from the hotel and told Alex where you were. He did the rest.'

'And putting me into your father's launch the other night? Was that part of the plan?'

'No. It just seemed like the safest thing at the time. It was quite a fight. I was on my way to meet Keef. He'd asked to meet at a bar near where you were. When I deposited you at Tre Oci, I went to the bar. Keef was there. Quite drunk.'

'It's a creepy feeling to know I've been watched, followed and deceived. I'm very disappointed. I trusted Alex when I thought he was being kind. And you've let me chatter away knowing far more than I could have guessed.'

'It's all over now. Keef is dead and so is Harold Foster. Whoever all these people were it's of no consequence to me any more.'

'I must get back to Burano,' Stella said. 'I need to think ... '

When Franco dropped her off at the waterbus station, he said, 'Will you be going to the police?'

She shook her head. 'This is all too confusing, I've no idea what I might say or how I might help. You're right. None of it would matter a jot except that someone has died and I ought not to be concealing the fact that I knew him. but thank you for being honest. The journey through the marshes was fantastic and the photos will be very helpful ... just a pity it's all happened in the wrong order.'

'I'm sorry for my part in all this. If you ever come back to Venice, you're welcome to spend the night here on the Lagoon. There's a couple of bunks and at night this place is magical. You can lie listening to the sound of the wind whispering across the salt marshes and, beyond you can sometimes hear the faint roar of the Adriatic, even louder when the surf breaks on bars of sand. I'll cook you some real Venetian specialities. There's sparkling white wine and all the grappa you want!'

In a sad way, it seemed to Stella like a beautiful dream.

10

'HEY, YOU LOOK GREAT, REALLY SMART, that really is a lovely cape, isn't it!' Irene ran her hands along Stella's shoulders and down her sides, cocking her head to one side as she appraised Stella's outfit. 'I've transformed you! Have you had something to eat? There's a great choice of bread, hot croissants, jam and honey? Coffee? Whatever you want. Do you know the breakfast room window overlooks the garden of the Peggy Guggenheim Collection? This is the authentic Venice.'

The room in which they stood had a small fireplace with a real fire flickering, exposed beams in the ceiling, and was lit by spotlights and wall-lights. As the windows were obscured by heavy drapes, it felt to Stella more like midnight than mid-afternoon. She was aware of other people moving about beyond the room in which they sat. Mobile phones trilled. Irene, dressed in a flowing robe and wearing an elaborate headdress settled into a large, square tan-coloured armchair opposite Stella who sat in one corner of a settee.

'Has it hit you yet, your father's death?' Stella said.

Irene looked up, slightly startled. 'That's nice of you to ask. I'm sad of course – he was my father, after all, but a distant man and one who never really paid much attention to me – to any of us. He gave such lovely hugs, though. I suppose he cared. Does your father give you big hugs?'

'He died when I was fourteen. I can remember him hugging me, though.'

Irene rose and came over to Stella, sat down beside her and embraced her. 'Hey, I'm so sorry that you had to go through all that.'

Stella said, 'It was a long time ago. I can hardly remember him ... '

Just then there came a knock on the door and a tall, angular man appeared with a nautical-looking sculpted white beard, sharp, bright eyes wearing a thick red sweater beneath a faded denim jacket. He was, Stella guessed, well into in his seventies, his face heavily lined but animated by a broad smile. He stood and beamed at Stella and waited until Irene turned to see him. 'Jack Kraft!' she cried, releasing Stella, rising and enveloping him.

'Jack, this is Stella, my personal assistant. This is Jack Kraft, one of Harold's oldest friends. I haven't seen Jack since I was a teenager! Jack, this is sad ... ' and she started to weep into Jack's neck while Jack stared over her shoulder at Stella, a raised eyebrow indicating something less than shared grief.

When at last Irene sat back next to Stella, she grasped one of her hands as if in support and Jack, slumping into the chair opposite the two women, said in a deep, gravelly London accent, 'Just flown in. What a shock. Great loss ... '

'Jack,' Irene said, 'I was telling Stella about Harold. I'm so grateful that she looked after Harold at the end – that he had a young woman to fuss over him. It's the way he would have chosen to go!'

'You bet!' said Jack, 'That was Harold's way. Loved a pretty face,' and he smiled at Stella.

'Jack exhibited with Harold for many years. Jack will agree with this, but Harold really had no idea about money. He always affected a sort of blank innocence when asked about exhibitions. Since his long-time dealer died he's been without proper representation. There hasn't been a formal exhibition of his work in years. Which is more than crazy. That's true, isn't it, Jack?'

Jack nodded, 'That's right. You couldn't budge him. A while ago, he said, looking round his studio, "Why do I do I keep all this stuff? I don't need the money! Now that I know what I want, I don't have to hold on to it quite so much."'

The fire in the grate crackled. Jack's comments didn't seem to have been what Irene wanted to hear.

'You see,' she started again, 'you probably don't know this but Harold was suffering from some sort of Alzheimer's ... '

Jack said, 'Alzheimer's?'

'You seem surprised.'

'He seemed very together when we last spoke ... ' Jack said.

Irene laughed. 'But he was obviously very, very confused. Why was he travelling here all alone for no apparent reason? You said he took a tumble in the airport, Stella? He never left his studio as a rule, hated travelling. Yet here he was in Venice, having told no one! I'm sure he had no idea where he was ... '

Jack said, 'The last time I visited him, oh, maybe five or six weeks ago, he did say "I don't remember so good anymore, d'ya mind?" and I said, "I don't either," and we laughed. But Alzheimer's?' and Jack looked at Stella and frowned.

'But, Jack, didn't he need help to finish his paintings?'

'Ridiculous!' Jack said, looking startled.

'I had it on good authority that an assistant or someone took a hand in helping him finish a piece of work ... '

Jack shook his head, 'No, no ... ' and laughed. 'You ... ' and he seemed to stop himself, then went on, 'I'll give you this, it's a tough call, to distinguish the finished from the abandoned!' and he rose. 'Irene, just touching base. I must find my room, have a wash. See you this evening, I guess?'

Irene enfolded him once more, Jack smiled at Stella once again and he left to find his room.

Irene moved back to her chair opposite Stella and took her hands.

'Jack really is old school, as in old ... You see, Harold lacked someone to look after his affairs,' she continued. 'I once tried to get a doctor to go and see him but he refused to let him in. An authority on ageing, he was the director of geriatric medicine somewhere. I was concerned about his competence. To handle his affairs properly, his finances.'

There was another silence.

'There were objections when I offered to become Harold's guardian. Jack might have been a part of that, I don't know. What's that legal term they have in Britain?'

'Power of attorney?'

'That's it. They said I had potential conflicts! That I had a loan from him to buy a house, and that there'd been additional sums paid to me from time to time. I'm his daughter! They weren't loans! They said, and I quote, ''She may or may not have an indebtedness to her father.'' And if I were appointed sole guardian, let along conservator, or what it's called here, I would have a "motive to encourage sales and to select an agent who will expedite sales." Too right I would! But they felt that such a strategy "most likely will not maximise prices," and thus not be best for Harold's assets. Yet they were killing the market for his work! Jack wouldn't understand that, of course. He hasn't sold anything much in decades. I don't think he was a good influence. Artwork should be offered on a controlled basis, at all times, and not held off, like they were doing. The absence of opportunities for folk to purchase is damaging to the prices because collectors lose interest. Flooding the market is harmful, of course. Am I boring you?'

Stella shook her head, and said, 'But Harold clearly had a different attitude.'

'Harold had Alzheimer's! How the hell could he decide what was best for his business?'

Stella, taken aback by the sudden outburst, said, 'I'm sorry,' but Irene had changed tack and now launched into a bitter tirade. 'I led a free-flowing, atypical life, but I'd never been accused of any wrongdoing. Not until all this recent business with Harold started. They dug out reports in newspapers ... Anyway, all that's in the past, I've put it behind me. I'm the sole beneficiary of Harold's will. They can't deny that. And we must get working. You wouldn't believe the people we have to contact. Seth is at the Embassy now sorting out the cremation business with the Consul. They've cut a lot of corners. It will be a feather in the cap for Venice – a tourist attraction, in a way. Not that they need it, I guess. I want a scattering of the ashes and a beautiful water-hearse. I don't think they've had a celebrity burial for many years. You're a lucky girl!'

Later that afternoon, I left the hotel and sat in a nearby cafe eating a toasted sandwich surrounded by laughing, chattering students. I still could not grasp Keef's death, that I had been with him that same night. I saw his face in front of me, the ridiculous hat and those tobacco-stained teeth. Then there was the encounter between Jack and Irene and her assumption that Foster could only have been suffering from Alzheimer's to have been travelling here, alone, with no apparent purpose. Only there was a purpose, and it concerned Keef. I knew I had to go to the police. Then, as if the thought of Keef had managed to stir his personal demons, my phone rang. It was Alice Casteret.

'Is that Stella Butler? I'm sorry to bother you. Franco gave me your number. Could you meet me in half an hour? I want to tell you something. Come to the Serra Margherita. It's a cafe at the end of the Viale Garibaldi, close by the Biennale Gardens. I'll be sitting outside.

The Serra Margherita was a tall, elegant glass-paned art nouveu structure with a wide expanse of green lawn in front. Stella could see no one outside. Inside, people were seated at wrought iron tables sipping coffee reading newspapers surrounded by plants and flowers. Natural light flooded in through the floor-to-ceiling windows that rose high above. After ten minutes, Alice appeared. She gestured to Stella to step outside. They found a table and Alice took out a packet of cigarettes and coughed.

'No?' she said, offering one to Stella, who shook her head. 'I shouldn't, I know.' She gave a throaty cackle of a laugh. She was shorter than Stella remembered with long dark brown hair framing a narrow, sharply featured face. She had deep, dark eyes and when she spoke, Stella detected a mixture of English/Italian in her accent.

'This place is like a haven to me. It's very old. Built over a hundred years ago. It's unlike anything else in Venice, made entirely of iron and glass, you see?' as she pointed up at the towering glass frontage. 'Once it cultivated plants for aristocratic ballrooms and such but now it's run as a cafe for the community, by volunteers who reintegrate former drug addicts. I know because I was in rehab and they helped me. Not drugs, drink. I come here to help sometimes, to pay back. A team of us restore gardens, plants, trees, all over the Lagoon. Local mothers come here after school to let the children play in the garden while they get plastered on prosecco cocktails! You'd like it. You are an ecologist? Franco said you were taking pictures of the marshes.'

'I'm doing some studying – or was.'

'Franco said that he told you about this man called Keef Cottesloe, that Franco had paid him to leave me alone. You knew Keef and he told you about coming to see me. And now Keef has been murdered.'

'Murdered?' Stella said.

'You don't know?'

'Keef's death was an accident. Surely.'

'No, no,' Alice said, shaking her head. 'Look,' and she proffered a Venice newspaper.

TRAGIC ex Moonstone drummer Keef Cottesloe may have been pushed to his death in Venice, it emerged last night. A 34-year-old man in Venice has claimed that he saw two men struggling on a bridge. 'I was walking home when I saw them on the Ponte degli Scalzi. I stopped and went to see if I could help. They seemed to be arguing about something. I told them to calm down but one of them started to push me and I fell to the floor where he kicked me. They started to fight and one of them pushed the other and he fell into the water. I ran away. Then I heard on the news that someone had died.'

'So now I am afraid for Franco and for Remigio.'

'Remigio?'

'He is my partner. We live on Mazzorbo, the island that adjoins Burano. You walk across the wooden footbridge to get to it. But I forget, you know this ... you've been there. I live there with his mother, Elena. You know Elena, too. You know everyone! Remigio took you out on the marshes. He behaved badly, and I'm sorry. I'll try and explain. Remigio is a very proud man, a native of Burano. He's too proud. He – we – were working on an old house in Mazzorbo, restoring it, so that we could live independently of Elena. The house was something he loved and he worked hard on it but we never had the finances to make a success of it. We owe Alex money as he lent us funds, well, lent *me* funds, to acquire the lease.

'Now Alex needed money and we didn't have a penny. The souvenir stall on Torcello makes nothing much and Remigio cannot fish as he once did. The only asset we had was Elena's collection of lace. Lovely table-cloths, old shawls, they were her mother's before her, some pieces were 200 years old and they were Remigio's inheritance. But we sold them to raise money to pay Keef. There was no other way. There were instant buyers. Alex was threatening us. Remigio has been angry ever since, angry about such lovely things being used to make Keef go away. Remigio and I argued and he blames me for it all and I agree, but I was scared. Now I can't contact him. I haven't seen Remigio for two days. His boat has gone. I am very afraid. You were on the Lagoon with Franco, what did he tell you? What do you know? I'm frantic. I can't think of anything ... '

'I don't see what I can tell you – '

'You were there in bed at Alex's on the night Franco went to see Keef; you were on the Lagoon with Remigio and then with Franco; you know Keef. I wanted to speak to you. So that you'll know that I have nothing to do with Keef. I must explain to you. I have to start somewhere, with someone. When Keef Cottesloe first came to me two weeks ago I panicked, because I was learning about something that had been hidden from me.'

'Hidden from you?'

'About who I am supposed to *be*. Who I am *not*? It's difficult.'

'Very difficult. I'm lost.'

'Why wouldn't you be? Okay. I live as Alice Casteret. My real name is Karen Michels. I came to Venice in 1979 from Salonica, in Greece, with my boyfriend; we were trekking through Bulgaria because my boyfriend's father knew someone of influence in Venice who could put us up. So, we found ourselves here and we set out in search of him, this friend, hoping to find him. I wandered away and got lost and eventually I returned to the station.

When I got there, my boyfriend had left without me. I had missed the train. We'd been arguing all the way from Greece so perhaps it was as well. I was young and I liked the twist of fate of finding myself in a city without any real reason for being there.

'I slept that night in the station. In the morning I went into the ticket office and argued for ten minutes before I got a refund on my ticket. Unbelievable! I now had some cash and could buy myself breakfast. It was like living in a dream, as though everything I had sought for all my life had crystallised into that moment, sitting in a café drinking Italian coffee and eating a croissant. I could have closed my eyes and drifted off into contented sleep there and then! But where to stay for the night? The address? The place we had originally set out to find, on the Giudecca, turned out to be a false trail.

'I then became part of the floating population of young people here who eke out a sort of hippy living. I changed my name. I always hated Karen so now I called myself Mystery Bouffe. Very silly. It was from a Mayakovski poem. That was what things were like then. I took menial jobs, did a little discreet begging, even some life-modelling. That's how I met Alex. I modelled for him once or twice. He took no notice of me other than to pay me and pass me on to other artists, but one day, out of the blue, he made me a proposition. I remember the day clearly.

'I called to ask for work one afternoon and when I entered the house it was empty but for him. That was unusual, because the place was never without half a dozen people, hanging out, passing through, eating and drinking. His attitude had changed and he was very kind to me and seemed interested in me. The proposition was a sort of exercise, he explained. A sort of living art event. That's how he described it. He wanted me to change my name again and to move into the house, the Tre Oci. He stressed that he wanted me to 'be' a new person, to change my identity, that he wanted to draw and paint me for some time as that person. I would have my own room and I could decide when I'd had enough.

'You must remember that I was without a past, having decided that my previous life was worthless. I was happy to adopt a new name, an exotic name! Alice Casteret was much better than Karen Michels and classier than Mystery Bouffe! Or so I thought. Later, he even produced a passport. I didn't have one – it had been stolen on the trip to get here. He then gave me an account book with money in it for me to spend. He would put money into it now and then whenever he sold a painting of me.

'I considered it a suitable way to live – in a city where masks are customary and usual. The arrangement worked well. Alex and I spent the days modelling and painting and when we finished work, we would go for drinks from bar to bar. It was a wonderful time. Thirty years ago the city was so different. I was Alice, the model and after a time everyone knew me as just that.

'Alex was tremendous fun, a compulsive talker and good-looking in a scruffy urchin sort of way. Very appealing to women. I never really knew about his background because I sensed he made a lot of it up, just as he made everything up about me. We were fictional characters. You wouldn't believe it, seeing him now, his tubby figure waddling between his canvas and his paint wagon with his silly black hat perched on top of his head. He looks more like an old-fashioned butcher wiping his hands down on his apron.'

Stella said, 'Didn't he ever explain whose identity it was you'd adopted?'

'That really wasn't an issue in my mind. I had no real sense that I had a stolen passport or that I was impersonating someone else. I was simply enjoying life. Alex and I became lovers for a time, and he created a new series of paintings – in his usual style – and made a lot of money from them. I shared in this good fortune. We had a son – Franco. I worked for other painters; Alex made sure that I got a great deal of work. Then, when Franco was six or seven, Alex and I broke up. It was amicable. Alex always was, probably still is, very keen on the opposite sex. You'll have experienced that, perhaps?

'I moved away, not far, to Burano and simply retained Alice's identity. When Franco was born, I needed medical insurance. There was some paperwork to do and some money was paid to the authorities by Alex, and suddenly I had become Alice Casteret, *officially*. The documents came through. It was a miracle.'

'Didn't you let your parents know where you were?'

'I was estranged from them. No one ever enquired after me and I had no desire to make contact myself. A city like Venice is a second home for people like me. But now, after all these years, everything rushes back and I am twenty-one again and guilty of committing a crime. It feels as fresh as that. When Keef appeared, I began to get a sense of – of exactly whose identity I had stolen. It appalled me. I had always believed that the new passport and the new name which Alex had given me were somehow not real, not those of a real person. When Keef appeared, he saw in me someone else, the lost girl. I felt I had been a party to a crime. A bigger crime.'

'Keef showed you the picture? The photograph of you and him?'

'She wasn't me, I'm certain. She looked very much like me but it was not me – that made it frightening, really frightening. Alex lied to me when he gave me her papers and effects. He said they came through the black market and that they had been partly manufactured and that the girl had probably never existed. But she clearly had existed. And she was so like me in appearance! That can't be a coincidence. It is an eerie feeling to know that you are living another person's life. My own background is so distant a memory, just the mere remnants of a forgotten life. I trusted Alex.'

'And Franco doesn't know this.'

'He has not been told, it never seemed necessary. But the girl, the real Alice – what happened to her? She was probably someone like me, a lost soul. I started to dream about her. I began to wonder about her, losing her name, losing her identity and I having stolen it.'

('Or losing her life?' Stella thought to herself. 'Did someone steal that?')

There was a silence between them. Alice lit another cigarette. She looked at Stella, who said, 'But after all this time, the penalty wouldn't be too great, surely? If you go to the authorities and explained yourself fully. I mean about the documents.'

'I asked Alex but he said I would be a fool to do that. He told me, "You have been living the life of another person for 30+ years, but even now the authorities will want to know what happened to her. You came by her effects – when? No date. You registered yourself some years later after having used her passport on and off for that time – she could have disappeared at any time during that period. You say I gave you the passport but there is no proof of that. Only that you have it, that you acquired it. You have taken money from an account of hers so that might well be seen as a motive on your part." But I took no money from her! Alex wasn't very kind to me. He said, "You may well claim that you let me persuade you but there is no proof of that. You didn't enquire at the time and now you are in a bad place ... "'

'Did he say he knew the girl?'

'He must have but he denies it.' She stared at Stella. 'I'm sorry, I'm sorry,' Alice said, rising to take Stella's arm. 'I don't care about Alex. It's Franco and Remigio that I'm bothered about. What happened when Franco met Keef? Did he tell you what happened? I feel so desperate, I can't bear to think of Franco and Remigio being involved in a murder.'

Stella said, 'Now look, Franco told me that he spoke to Keef, that Keef was happy to accept money from him and that he then left. I was taken to Alex's that night, you remember, you found me there. I didn't hear from Keef again and then I heard he had drowned. Remigio will have had nothing to do with that, I'm certain. But what can I do? Why are you telling me all this?'

Alice said, 'I feel responsible for Keef Cottesloe's death. He would be alive now if I hadn't taken the girl's name. But I can't tell Franco. I can't tell Remigio. I can't even find them. I'm afraid of Alex, that he will abandon me in order to protect himself. You understand that I am not this woman Keef sought, that I am nothing to do with Harold Foster. I hope you believe me.'

'I believe you.' Stella almost added, "But do you have a gold tooth ... ?" Instead, she said, 'I'll do what I can. I'll try and help you.'

Alice said, 'Did you sleep with Alex?'

'No.'

'But I imagine he tried?'

'Not really. He just dressed me up as Salome. He's still trying to give people new identities.'

'I feel sorry for him,' Alice said. 'He never moved on. He remained here while the Venetians we once lived amongst all fled or faded away or died: the bohemians and the hippies and rock and roll people. Nothing remains of that world but Alex is still here. He fits in perfectly with the shallow characters who own expensive homes here and the tourists who come for the Carnival or the artists who fill the galleries full of horrible paintings and worse. He had ability but he didn't develop it, he's lazy inside.'

'I feel bad about something,' I said. I went to see Elena after the last no-show by Remigio. She was very kind to me and she gave me this. [I took out the lace fisherman.] I don't know why she gave it to me. I owed Remigio money for taking up his time but she refused it. I don't feel I should keep this, it's beautiful and worth a lot of money. Would you take it back?'

Alice looked at it and smiled and said, 'Of course not. She would be offended and so would I. She had her reasons for giving it to you, I'm sure, and what it's worth is up to you. When you come here again you can bring her something of yours that you value, she would be thrilled. I must go and you must be busy. Please tell me anything that you find.'

We parted by the Giardini waterbus stop as the evening light began to fade across the Lagoon. Back at the hotel I spoke to Seth, who told me Irene was sleeping. 'An early night before the big occasion.' We exchanged notes and discussed the morning to come, after which I retreated to my room and lay on my bed, attempting to come to terms with had happened that day.

I felt ashamed of my own behaviour – getting drunk two nights in a row and then playing the fool with Alex wearing a ridiculous dress and dancing about just hours after Keef must had drowned somewhere. Alex's advice that I tell no one about my connection with Keef now looked calculating, as though he was manipulating me. But why?

That Keef had died, the realisation of it, kept creeping up on me. I'd hardly met him but his bizarre story had eaten into my life somehow. I could see him now wearing that hat and laughing. I held back from googling his name but I looked up Mario de Maria and the history of the House. That at least was true and, in an odd way, I was relieved. Mario had existed. I'd been half afraid he'd been invented by Alex. But my delight at the House had faded and I now felt angry at my gullibility. What should I do? What did I imagine I was dealing with?

11

THE NEXT MORNING FOSTER'S FUNERAL took place in the small Jewish chapel in the Giovanni e Paolo hospital. The service was brief, broken occasionally by recorded music that, according to Irene, Harold had 'loved'. There were no speeches. Afterwards, among the ill-at-ease throng standing outside in the Campo Santi Giovanni e Paolo I shuttled between guests, argued with photographers, and thanked the Rabbi. I arranged for the collection of Harold's ashes with the funeral director before helping to direct everyone onto the decorated launches that would take them across the Lagoon to the funeral lunch.

Crossing the water with the gusting wind driving low clouds towards the distant mountains, the mood of the assembled mourners lifted and a loud chatter drowned even the rumble of the launch's engines. Finally, we drifted slowly along Torcello's main canal leading to the Cipriani's landing stage close by the small bridge. Curious tourists took pictures of us as we glided by. Inside, as the last of the guests took their seats at their tables, as Irene stood and began a welcoming speech, I slipped away, walked along to where the souvenir stands were situated, where I had encountered Alice. Her stall was shut and tightly enclosed in its tarpaulin wrapping.

Later, the guests gathered outside the restaurant ready to leave.

119

Photographs were taken and a television crew began interviewing Irene standing alongside various distant relatives and Venetian dignitaries. I waited by the official launches at the landing stage, smiling, settling people into their places. At last Irene joined them and we set off back across the Lagoon. Irene sat next to me. She was elated and said, 'Harold would have loved it! I'm a little high, this is all too much,' and she gazed out across the grey, clouded Lagoon with tears in her eyes. I could only think of Alice and her strange tale. I felt a sense of bewilderment at my predicament while at the same time wondering, as I considered the lavish arrangements for Harold's death, what sort of funeral poor Keef would get.

When the launch deposited us on the Hotel Bauer landing stage, I walked with Irene to the hotel lobby although I was anxious to hurry away. Irene put a hand to her forehead. 'My head's swimming again. The ashes scattering should be over by around 11.30 or so on Sunday morning but we need to finalise the permits. Maybe you could come back in a little while? Text me, sweetie. We're going to have a quiet supper tonight at Harry's Bar. We'd love you to come along.'

My head was swimming, too. I met with the funeral directors and worked for an hour or so, checking the ashes casket, checking on the submission to the relevant authorities for permission to disperse the ashes and the place of dispersal. It was a maze of civil codes, mortuary officials, times of collection, delivery, the ordering of yet more launches. There seemed hardly enough time for such things to be processed but the mention of Harold's name seemed to make many things possible.

In the late afternoon, I texted Irene to say I was very tired and that I wouldn't make it to Harry's Bar. But I also needed to be sure Irene didn't come banging on my door and find me, so I left the hotel and its oppressive luxury. I needed fresh air and a clear head, but no sooner had I stepped out of the hotel lobby, than my phone rang.

'May I speak to a Miss Stella Butler? This is Donato calling from Polizia di Stato in Mestre. Could you tell me your whereabouts, please?'

'I'm close by the Bauer Hotel,' I said.

'We would like you to help us with an enquiry. It will not take long. Could you come to Piazzale Roma and wait by the bus station ticket office? Someone will collect you.'

He wouldn't explain any further. I hurried through the half-deserted alleyways feeling relieved. I would tell Donato what I knew about Keef. Everything was starting to unravel.

At the police station, I was ushered into a small room with a large dark glass screen dominating one wall, and told that someone would be with me shortly to ask me some questions. I sat at the table just as the room went completely dark. I then saw that the screen was in fact a window through which I could now see, brightly lit, another smaller room containing a table and some chairs. As I watched, a door in the room beyond opened and a man stepped into view. I stared in horror at the familiar, goatee-bearded figure as he pulled up a chair and sat at the table. Simultaneously, the lights came on in my room and went out in the room beyond and I found myself staring back at my own shocked face in the mirror-screen. 'Keef,' I said, 'Keef Cottesloe! That was Keef Cottesloe, surely?' as a flustered-looking policeman hurried in saying, 'Mi scusi, I'm sorry, there's been a mistake. Please, come with me.'

'Was that a film?' I said.

'Please, come with me.'

Stella tried to stand but she found her legs were trembling and she had to sit down again. 'Can I have a glass of water?' she asked. 'That was Keef Cottesloe wasn't it? I can't believe it.'

The policeman called for some water and she heard raised voices down the corridor outside. A man dressed in a well-tailored suit entered carrying a glass of water and sat down opposite her. He smiled. They looked at one another and Stella saw again the familiar sharp-featured face, a slight smile on his lips.

'Donato,' she said, 'I don't feel very well.'

'Please accept my apologies. My colleagues thought you were a witness brought in to identify the gentleman concerned. It was a mistake.'

'It *is* Keef, isn't it? This is very confusing. It's not some sort of film or video is it?'

'No, it was a stupid thing to do, to shock you like that.'

'Is it him?' she said.

'Yes, it's Mr Cottesloe.'

'I don't understand what's happened. They said he'd drowned in a canal.'

'Terrible mistake. The body found in the canal was in possession of personal items that suggested it was Mr Cottesloe. There was a physical resemblance but the information was wrong. This morning, Mr Cottesloe appeared in this office. You know him, of course? He asked to speak to you.'

Keef was sitting in the airless, bare room she had observed earlier. As she entered, he clapped his hands together like a large child and smiled and said, 'Bloody hell. Am I glad to see you!' Despite herself, she began to weep, so he reached out and tried to give her a hug but she slipped past him to sit at the table. He watched her for a moment, then said, 'Come on, Stella, it's not your bloody fault. Look, I'm sorry to drag you into all this but I needed someone to help get me out of here. I don't know the ropes and I haven't a bloody penny.'

She blew her nose and sipped at a glass of water.

'I'm sorry about this blubbing, it's just a shock to see you alive. You don't look very well.'

'I've had a rough couple of days. They're hanging on to all my personal stuff at the moment. Don't ask me why.'

She stared at his large, unkempt face with its bemused expression and she remembered the last time they'd spoken, when his dogged pursuit of Alice had angered her. Something of that ire now resurfaced. It relieved her, that she could feel angry at him.

'Why did they say it was you in the canal when no one had even identified you? How irresponsible is that, to let everyone think you'd drowned?'

Keef was silent for a moment, as if allowing the idea to sink in before exclaiming, 'You thought I was dead! *That's* what all this is about!'

'It was all over the papers. It's on television,' she said. 'Didn't the police tell you?'

'They haven't told me a thing. I still don't think they know who I really am! I'm in the papers? What papers?'

'All of them. Your songs are on the radio, too.'

'Songs?'

'Your records, the things you played for me.'

'Early stuff? Not stuff with Ozzy! That bugger ... '

'What *difference* does it make which songs they are!' she said as angry tears welled up again inside her. 'I can't remember the blasted titles ... !'

'You mean, people have written my obits?' His face lit up, his eyes widened and he laughed. 'Wow! Have you got any with you? My God!' and he laughed again. 'No wonder you looked shocked!'

'I have to say it, because it sounds a bit unkind after what you've been through, but you've really caused some trouble here,' she said. 'It isn't anything to laugh about,' but she did laugh and cry simultaneously.

He sat down opposite her and laughed with her, shaking his head. 'Can't help it! Everyone thought I was dead! No wonder I look so bloody rough!'

'But what exactly happened to you?'

'That's a story! When that fight broke out and you disappeared, I wandered about, looking for a bar where I was supposed to meet up with someone.'

'Franco Casteret?' she said.

'How'd you know that?'

'An educated guess.'

'I think you're a bit psychical. Well, after the meeting, I was on my way back to the van and I was somewhere near the bridge leading across to Mestre when this big bloke jumped me. Gyppo-type. He threatened me with a knife, took my bum-bag, wallet and money then took a swing at me. We scuffled a bit and I hit him and he hit me, then he ran off. I was concussed. I don't really remember much after that. I think I got on a bus and then just wandered back to the van somehow and then collapsed. Spark out. I slept a day or so and just sort of drifted. See?' and he indicated a bruise at the back of his neck. 'Concussion. Not the first time. I fell off the stage in Nuremberg once and they hauled me back up and I continued playing for a whole set, had no memory of it at all! Didn't know where I was until afterwards when this gorgeous bird – '

'Could we concentrate on the here and now?' Stella said.

'Right, sorry. When I came to I realised I had to tell someone so I went to the police and said I'd been mugged. They produced all the stuff which had been stolen from me, money, wallet. It was all in the bum-bag. Word of advice, by the way: never use a bum-bag. You lose everything in one go!

Anyway, I said, "That's all mine" – and they bloody arrested me! The other bloke must have collapsed later and fallen into the water or something. They must've found my stuff on him. My travel card! Had a picture of me. They must have thought it matched. You wouldn't bloody believe it! He was an ugly looking bugger, too.'

'I'm very sorry,' Stella said and began to weep again.

'Sorry for what? I'm just happy you're here.'

'But I still can't believe that no one came to identify you.'

'Don't rub it in, girl,' he said. 'Someone would have made it eventually.'

'Not that I'm anyone to talk. I was very selfish.'

'I was dead, what could you do? Not your problem, lover.'

'Although it is now, apparently.'

'I was just hoping you might do the business and get me out of here. Stella, I'm clueless.'

'Do you know what the police are planning? Have you spoken to a lawyer?'

He shook his head. 'I've not understood half of what they've said so far.'

She stood up. 'I'd better start the ball rolling. The British Embassy should be able to help. I'll call them. Isn't there anybody back home who might help?'

'The ex-wife. Not sure if she's not in the States, though.' As she moved to the door, he said, 'I could do with a cup of tea by the way. I did ask, earlier. Got lost in translation.'

'I think we'll concentrate on getting you out of here first,' Stella said.

An hour later, seated in Keef's camper van, Stella listened as he talked to friends on her phone, explaining, shaking his head in bemusement, guffawing with laughter. 'I know, I know! Fucking unbelievable!' When he sat down opposite her and returned her phone, his face was red with excitement.

'When all this has been sorted, I'm back on track!' he said. 'I've got a stonkin' record deal, a bloody tour with Ozzy Osbourne! Bastard wrote a song about me, thinking I'd popped off! It's like Buddy Holly, this, only in reverse!'

The phone rang again and Stella handed it back to him but he shook his head. 'No, no ... We'll be here all week on that thing. You need to get off. There's a pay-phone on the site – I'll get on it later, I've got a sack of change.'

'It might take a while before you can leave Italy. They may still charge you after the inquest. It was murder, originally – only *yours*. Now it's someone else's.'

'Oz's got me some legal help. Someone's coming later today from a top Italian firm. There'll be no problem. Really. Look, I can't thank you enough. I know I'm not your favourite person, but –'

She shook her head. She said, 'Keep using the phone for a while, I'd like to lie down, I'm tired. I've not had a lot of sleep.'

She lay down on Keef's bunk, closed her eyes and drifted into a reverie punctuated all the while by Keef's hoarse voice drifting in from the front of the van where he sat laughing and shouting, 'Elated, over the moon! Fucking Ace!'

It was two o'clock in the afternoon when I awoke to silence. Keef was nowhere to be seen. I found my phone on the front seat of the van and checked my messages again. I tried to call Franco but my phone was dead. Keef had used up all the credit. He had, I surmised, gone off to find the pay-phone with his bag of change. I squeezed myself into the van's cramped chemical toilet and found myself looking at a photo of Alice pinned on the back of the door. It looked like the cropped photo Keef had shown me earlier only this was the full picture, with more people in it. As I stared at it, I heard the camper van door bang open.

She called out, 'I'm using the loo!'

She found him unpacking groceries, the kettle boiling and cups prepared.

'I'm sorry about the phone,' he said. 'I owe you. Fancy a cuppa?'

'No, I'm going,' she said. 'But I want to clear something up. Don't ask me how, but I know that you were offered a bribe to leave Alice alone. Why did you take the money?'

'A bribe?' He made a low humming sound to himself and gave Stella a sheepish look. 'A bribe. I suppose it was. Did the police say it was a bribe?'

'No, they know nothing about it, but they're puzzled that you had some much money on you, it looks a bit suspicious. I'm just surprised you took it, after all you'd been through, after all it meant to you.'

'I was broke. Harold had gone and the story looked a hard one to prove. Franco said to me, "The Foster family won't be interested in your story and you'll end up getting fried legally." I thought, "I gotta get out of here, it's ripping me to pieces." If your confidence takes enough knocks, it's damaging, very mentally damaging. So I decided to go. But fate nailed me down here.'

'Well, I'm relieved you've given up on this search for the "lost love" because you're wrong. I've met her and talked to her.'

'You've met Alice!'

'She really isn't the woman you thought, take my word for it. The truth is less appealing than the myth and she's not mysterious any more. Think about it. Surely you've enough material for your book without dragging a real, ageing troubled woman into it? The quest is all.'

'The Quest! That's a stonking good title. "The Quest is All!"'

Keef sat down on the narrow, low bench that ran down one side of the van and lit a cigarette. 'I'm lining up a music deal, the songs are selling. I'm writing new stuff. It's all to do with her. The Quest ... ' and he seemed to have drifted away into a musical reverie.

'Can I make something else clear, Keef? The police will probably ask you about meeting Franco. They'll then probably question him. When they do he'll tell them that he recognised you and approached you as a fan. He'll do you no favours. He won't mention anything about handing over any money. You chatted and then parted. I'm only telling you this because you might have said something else which would contradict him. They're investigating a possible murder, remember, something you seem to forget. So, any small deviation will look odd. I would tread carefully. And I'd come up with a good reason why you were carrying so much cash.'

'You should be a lawyer,' he said.

'I should be somewhere else. I'm in the middle of overseeing a funeral. Or the end of one.'

'Bloody good job it's not mine! And you're right. I took his money so I shouldn't be here. Stella, you've been a sport. I've got to give you something,' and he disappeared inside the van, returning with a small, white box. 'Something for you to remember me by. My last drummer bear. Remember? I was the Bear! Just like me, wind him up and watch him go!'

Stella took it and said, 'That's very sweet of you, thank you. But there's something else I would *really* like – that photo in the toilet. The Alice one.'

He frowned but went back inside again and returned with it.

'This is what started everything, isn't it?' he said and handed it to her.

'This is a bigger print, though. The other picture, the one of you and Alice that you carry about, it's this one cropped. This one's got more people in it. Who are they?'

'That's Harold Foster standing in the background with someone, not sure who, looking down at some paintings stacked against the studio wall. It was in the studio, in the house where she died. I never worked out where it was.'

Stella stared at the 'someone': slimmer and with a head of dark hair just like his son, Franco. It was Alex in the House with Three Eyes. She put the photo in her bag.

At the door of the van, Keef said, 'I'd walk you to a bus stop but there's some press coming!'

'Are you sure you're allowed to talk to the newspapers?'

'You know, you'd make a bloody good manager. You don't fancy the job?'

'I meant the police might object to you talking to journalists.'

'It's just a couple of interviews. Things are moving fast. I can't believe the way it's all changed in just a few hours. I'd dreamt of it, but wow! the thought of it knocks me sideways. I would have liked to put it all back together but then we wouldn't be where we are today. So, fate – the destiny of my life, meeting other people – it came to what it is. Am I making any sense?'

'None at all.'

'Good, must be doing something right!'

Outside the camper van site Stella found the bus stop for Venice. Within minutes, however, a car drew up and she saw Donato gesturing to her. She climbed inside. He smiled.

'You haven't been watching me have you?' she said.

He said, 'Could I ask you some questions?'

'Go ahead,' Stella said as they accelerated away.

'How do you know Mr Cottesloe?

'I've met him here a couple of times but I don't really know him. He called me on Harold's phone an hour after I landed.'

'You didn't mention it when we were at the hospital.'

'I did. I told you someone had called me, that I wanted you to have the phone, but you said to give the phone to his relatives. You said it wasn't your jurisdiction.'

'This man Keef knew Harold Foster's daughter?'

'No.'

'But he knew Harold Foster?'

'Yes.'

'Do you know what he wanted with Harold Foster?'

'He was in Venice hoping to find a girl he'd met here thirty years ago. He thought Harold might be able to help.'

'Why?'

'Because she might have been one of his daughters.'

'One of Cottesloe's daughters?'

'One of Foster's.'

'And where is this woman? The one Keef was seeking?'

'I have no idea. I don't think he was successful.'

'You thought Keef Cottesloe was dead.'

'Of course. It was in all the newspapers.'

'You didn't make contact with the authorities when you heard he had died?'

She shook her head.

'You heard he had drowned?'

She nodded.

Donato said, 'A man is thought to have been drowned – murdered – and no one knows what has happened. You know him, but you stay away.' He looked perplexed. 'My colleagues were puzzled as to why you didn't come forward when you heard that Mr Cottesloe had drowned in the canal.' He waited. 'It's not a normal reaction.'

'But not a crime. I didn't know him well. I couldn't see how I could help. I assumed his family would come and claim him,' she said. 'The murder business came afterwards. I was going to tell you when I came to the police station, but it turned out Keef wasn't dead at all.

'He doesn't know you well but he called you when he was in trouble.'

'That was a surprise.'

'When was the last time you spoke to Mr Cottesloe before today?'

'Two or three days ago in a square somewhere near Ca D'oro.'

'On the night he was supposed to have drowned. Do you know anyone else in Venice who knows Mr Cottesloe?''

'No.'

'You know of a Mr Franco Casteret?'

'Franco?'

'You are friends with Mr Casteret?'

'I've known him for a couple of days.'

'Mr Casteret was seen with Mr Cottesloe that evening.'

'Someone recognised Franco?'

'Venice is a big place, but it is also a small place, if you understand me. It was a bar where local people go. We called Franco in and he said, "I bought him a drink because I recognised him." Question. Why didn't he go to the police when news of Keef's death was made public? No answer. But that is a question for later. At about the time Keef "died" Franco says he was in another bar. How did you meet Franco?'

'In an art gallery when I first arrived.'

'Franco is a painter?'

'No, his father is. It was his father's gallery. Alex Osbourne, the Three Eyes Gallery.'

'And you've known Alex for how long?'

'Only since I arrived here, three or four days ago.'

'Did you know that Franco knew Mr Cottesloe?'

'I think he'd met him but I don't think he actually knew him.'

'So, how did you know the two men were acquainted?'

'Did I say that? I suppose I did. Franco mentioned it when the news came out about Keef's death. I'm sorry, that slipped my mind.'

'*What* did Franco tell you about meeting Mr Cottesloe?'

'As you said, he recognised him as a rock musician and he bought him a drink. So who *did* drown?' Stella asked.

Donato shrugged. 'No one has identified the body yet. The news that it was Cottesloe means people think the problem is solved. A dead man appears in a canal. We think he is Cottesloe. We are wrong, but before we can discover this, a letter comes saying Z fought with Y and maybe caused his death. Then Cottesloe appears saying, I am alive, I was mugged by Y and maybe hit him but he was alive when I last saw him – and he had all my money etc. Cottesloe was robbed of a considerable amount of money. More money than a man living like a vagrant in a camper van who couldn't afford a mobile phone might be expected to have. So, we have an unidentified dead man, plus a man who claims he was mugged by him, and a letter from a second man Z who says he also fought with Y before he died. My suspicion is that the letter is a hoax, sent by someone who was drawn to the issue by the publicity. It makes no sense otherwise. But we must investigate. My main problem is identifying the dead man. Who is he? Someone who looks like Cottesloe, heavy build, long hair, older, "brutto". The two men were similar and so any eye-witnesses maybe mixed them up.' Donato was silent again, then said: 'We would like you take a look at the dead man.'

'Me? Why?'

'Just in case ... '

'In case of what?'

'In case you know him. You seem to know everyone.'

'Is that supposed to be funny?'

'I am serious. Wherever I turn in this investigation, I find you. It's nice in a way, but ... '

'I'm sure I wouldn't know him.'

'It's just a request. I have a feeling. You're leaving Venice when?'

'I'm flying home as soon as I finish my work here. I'm helping with a funeral. '

'A funeral?'

'Harold Foster's. The artist.'

'You said you were a student?'

'I did.' She shrugged. 'Part-time unfortunately. Foster's daughter asked me to help her. She's here arranging his cremation. I'm working for her.'

Donato laughed. 'You see? I find you everywhere! A trip to a morgue will be a natural follow-up. Why not?'

We left his car at Piazzale Roma and took the police launch to the Giovanni e Paolo hospital, and I couldn't help but reflect on what the past week had brought. Across the square past the statue of Colleoni and over the little bridge was the bar where I'd first met Keef, and here I was returning to the spot where Harold Foster's body had been deposited.

We descended to where the hospital mortuary was situated and I waited, heart pounding, as we paused opposite the shelf upon which the dead man lay.

'Have you looked at a corpse before?' Donato asked.

'Yes, my father's,' I said.

They pulled the shelf out. I stared down at Remigio Dei Rossi.

12

THAT NIGHT I HARDLY SLEPT AT all, turning scenarios over and over in my mind. Alice's partner, Elena's son, had now died as a result of his fighting Keef. Why had they met in the first place? Because Remigio was angry about the money he'd had to raise to get rid of Keef? If that was so, I was once again concealing potentially shattering information from Donato, as well as conniving in Franco's alibi and deceiving Irene.

I spent the next morning meeting and greeting various elderly guests arriving from the Marco Polo Airport for the next day's ashes scattering and settling them into hotels. I finally caught the waterbus alone and crushed into my seat by crowds of chattering and laughing commuters and tourists, I let my thoughts drift aimlessly out across the water. There was something soothing about watching the routine movements of the men at each landing stage swinging barriers open, ushering people on and off while the boat shuddered towards huge wooden piles, rocking and rolling, bumping and grinding. Every now and then there came a whirring, rumbling sensation beneath my feet as the boat's engine churned up the dark water disturbing the green hair-like tresses of waterweeds just beneath the surface. The watery turmoil mirrored my feelings, and I would have been content to just sit and watch, but I had an appointment to see Irene in her suite back at the Bauer Hotel.

When I entered, I saw that a projector had been set up on a small table. Irene was in an odd mood, and I felt uncomfortable. She indicated for me to sit down on a sofa. 'I wanted to show you something,' was all she said at first before setting in motion a power-point display of photos of Harold Foster at various different Venice Biennale exhibitions along with images of some of his painting.

She stopped the display when it reached a small painting of a girl lying on her back on an unmade bed. I just had time to glance at it when Irene said,

'You wouldn't believe it, but when I was young, I exerted an extra-ordinary seductive power over men and women. I was lean and elegant with dark hair and enormous deep blue eyes. I was a dream for any creative artist ... savage, wild, romantic and completely shameless! Not that you'd know it in Harold's pictures of me. I've been painted by some of the greats, you wouldn't know that, either. Have you heard of Balthus? He was a great friend of Harold's. His portrait of me is owned by some private collector in America. It's worth millions. I saw it recently at an exhibition in the Guggenheim gallery in New York. It's strange, like being one of those lovely characters painted by Titian or Goya, up there for people to stare at. A great painter steals your soul.'

'Not that you'd know that Harold was a great artist after reading all this stuff about these children he had, or it's claimed he had – it's all rubbish. "My Life as Harold Foster's Love-child" – that kind of thing. When you have a bunch of offspring by so many wives and girlfriends and when only a handful of them are permitted to have your phone number, speculation runs away with itself. My mother once said: "You might have a love affair with Harold if that's what you wanted but he hated responsibility and it would have been crazy to have children with him."

'My mother was an artist Harold had a long affair with in the 1950s. They lived together in a house in Sussex which she was given life-use of by Harold when he left her; they never married. Once the first flush of excitement had passed, it was a miserable existence for her. Harold was already blatantly eyeing up other women and made very little secret of his infidelities. He was reckless with money, stayed away for days at a time gambling and could be brutal during their frequent rows. Once after a particularly vicious fight he pushed my mother into the hall of the seedy hotel where they were staying. She was completely naked, but he refused to let her back in.

'When he left, I didn't see him for years. We went back to the States where my mother came from, Chicago. Harold and I had never lived in the same city before but I was in London when I was sixteen looking for work as a fashion model and I went and sat for him. That's how I got to know him, as a father. I simply took my clothes off and sat on a sofa in the studio when he asked. It never occurred to me to be ashamed. It was a way of simply being with him. It wasn't as if I was posing for Playboy or peddling my wares in a red-light district. After that I saw him every few years – sometimes by arrangement, sometimes not – but never in a nice, regular fashion.

'I suppose I should have hated him but he acted on his feelings, took what he wanted and I accepted that. Harold eschewed morality. His only moral defence – the one always made by intensely selfish people – was that he was being "honest". "I am what I am. This is what I like to do. If you want to fit in with that, you're very welcome to come into my life. But don't try and make me something I'm not." I understood that form of selfishness and I respected it.'

I could only murmur something in the affirmative. It was't really a conversation we were having. She turned to look at the small painting that we'd paused at in the display.

'This is one of Harold's earliest, done some time back when he was staying in Venice in the 1980's. It's owned by someone you know.'

'Someone I know?' I said. I looked again at the picture.

'He lives on the Giudecca. He's called Alex Osbourne.'

'Alex?'

'When you were out yesterday he called here. He said he knew you and that he'd even met Harold way back in the eighties. He'd been given this painting so it's not catalogued, it's quite a find.'

I turned once again to look at the painting. The naked girl was sprawled on her back, her face turned away and her eyes closed. The picture made me feel uneasy, even a little queasy. I could see the girl's rib cage quite clearly beneath her small, almost childlike breasts. The colours were vibrant: scalding oranges against cold blues; warm yellows against slate purples. They lent the picture a garish, almost nightmarish quality. The girl lay as if splayed out for inspection: it was quite clinical, almost as though she was on a surgical bed. She could have been asleep or she could have been dead. The image seemed to me cold and ruthless and merciless.

'He's got a photo of Harold with the model herself along with the painting. Here,' and she handed it to me. 'It establishes the picture's provenance.'

Once again I saw the small, thin face of Keef's Angel, the original Alice. I realised it must have been taken at the same time as the photo Keef had shown me, in the same studio as the one in Keef's photo. Those windows, that distinctive view. I knew where it was because I'd been there. Alex's studio in the Tre Oci. I even had my own photograph of the place.

'There's a letter. Seth's having it checked. But I'm curious, Stella. How did you get to know Alex?' Irene was saying. I continued staring down at the photo, my mind trying to piece together a variety of possibilities.

'I bumped into him when I first got here. He approached me in a square near his gallery for some reason. I didn't know about his connection with Harold. I didn't know that he'd been in Alex's studio. I would have thought they were worlds apart. Certainly, as artists.'

'You've seen Alex's work?'

'Yes, in his 3-Eyes gallery. He specialises in large paintings of half-naked young girls.'

'By the sound of it you don't approve of him.'

'I find his work questionable. I suppose I don't really know him very well.'

'Really?' Irene laughed. 'But well enough to dress up for him?' and with a sort of magician's flourish she produced a large photograph of me lying on Alex's couch wearing the Salome dress.

I was shocked. 'Where did that come from?' I asked, although the answer was obvious.

Irene said, 'Alex left it here. Don't get angry! Please! But you're just such a mystery, you must admit it. You meet up with Harold at the airport, by chance. After he dies, you have his phone, by chance. You then meet up with Alex, a painter and the only man in Venice who knew Harold, again by sheer chance. Whatever you think of him and his work, Alex said great things about you. When he knew you were helping me out with Harold's funeral arrangements, he thought it a great idea if he made contact with me given their shared past. The painting was a key. What a find! And there's more. He's invited Seth and me and one or two other special guests over for a quiet celebration after the ashes scattering to his wonderful place on the Giudecca, a sort of post-wake memorial with light refreshments and some music. He'll need a little help with putting things together, some expert planning, so I suggested you'd go over and lend a hand. I'm going to show this short photo résumé of Harold's painting career. This little painting of Harold's will be on display! It reminds me of things he did of me! What do you think?'

'Are you including my photos in the picture show?' I asked.

'I said don't get angry, Stella! Here,' and she handed me the print. 'Tear it up.' She then reached out and hugged me. 'You shouldn't be so self-conscious! You're a good-looking girl. It soon fades. I know. I'm jealous! Fancy, though, you're wearing a dress that Rita Hayworth wore! I'm really, really jealous. I loved her pictures. I wanted to look like her! Off you go now, he's waiting for you. You can tell him off for showing me the photo!'

It might have been better to have refused but I realised it afforded me a chance to say one or two things to Alex before I decided on whether or not to go to Donato and tell all. So many conflicting stories, so many lies: everything that had happened, all that was happening, appeared to revolve around Alex. I went back to my hotel room and changed into my old clothes so that at least I felt more like myself again.

When Alex opened the front door Stella thought he looked flustered, even ill. He gave her no greeting but turned and hurried away and she followed him, her intention to stand and vent her anger at him thwarted by the sight of his ungainly, limping, figure disappearing within.

'Let's go to the kitchen, the studio is a bloody mess,' he said over his shoulder. Once there, he lowered himself onto a stool and, before she could say anything, began to speak. 'Did you know that Irene is coming with guests tomorrow after the ashes scattering? I thought you could advise me. How many will there be?'

Perhaps he wasn't ill but anxious, she thought. Perhaps, she mused, he was afraid of something. 'You look tired,' he said. 'Can I get you a drink?'

'I'm probably still in shock.'

'About Cottesloe. Of course. What a bloody shambles. They're playing his awful music again on the radio. The police will look very stupid ... '

'The dead man is Remigio.'

Alex stared at her as if he hadn't heard her.

'I identified him last night.'

'You've been speaking with the police?

'Obviously'

'Does Alice know?'

'I've no idea.'

'Did the police ask you anything?'

'How I knew Remigio and you.'

'Me?'

'That's how I met Remigio, through you. You arranged my trip with him, on the marches.'

'Did they ask any questions about me?'

'Why would they do that?'

'But you mentioned me?'

'I just told you I did. I said you were a painter and that you owned a gallery. You're lucky. I could have said that it was you who sent Franco off with all that money found on poor Remigio.'

'Who told you that?'

'Franco. And that you know Keef Cottesloe.'

'I don't know Cottesloe from Adam.'

'You're in a picture together in your studio.' She took out the photo Keef had given her and handed it to him. 'Here.' Alex stared at it, turned it over as if in search of some clue before handing it back at Stella. 'Keef gave it to me yesterday. He didn't recognise you but I did. It is you, isn't it? In your studio. It couldn't be anywhere else, those tall windows looking out onto the Giudecca. They're in all the paintings.'

'There were all sorts of people in and out of the place in those days, over forty years ago. It was open house.'

'So you know the date? It's similar to a photo Irene showed me yesterday, one that you used to prove you owned a painting. You're in that one, too: you, Keef – and Harold Foster. You told Irene that you knew Foster well.'

'I didn't say I knew him *well* ... '

'Enough for him to give you a priceless picture. Yet you carried on with *me* as if you didn't know him at all. It was the same with Keef. You pretended *not* to know anything about him when I asked for advice, when I was very upset and thought he'd drowned. I thought we had some sort of friendship ... but nothing makes any sense now. All those silly lies about having a wife in Perugia and a daughter whose scarf/jacket you gave me.'

'I've a cupboard full of them – I give one to all the girls ... '

'Can't you understand? I'm *very* angry,' Stella said. 'Franco tells me I've been followed from the moment I arrived here! You ruined my work here, telling Remigio I knew Keef so that he behaved badly. Why did you do that? Don't try and answer, I couldn't care less. But I've been *used*.'

'Used?'

'Showing Irene those photographs you took of me, humiliating me and invading my privacy? I dressed up because you asked me to, not to have my image pimped about so that you could smarm your way into Irene's company.'

'Smarm ... as in obsequious, oily and greasy?'

'And another thing, about Foster's painting. If the model is Foster's daughter, which Keef claims she is, and I'm more and more inclined to believe him, then she's also Irene's half-sister. Don't you think she should know who she's looking at?'

'Sounds like one of Cottesloe's flights of fancy. Have you listened to any of his songs?'

'None of this is *funny* ... '

'I haven't a clue as to who the model was or is.'

'Her name was Alice Casteret – the same name as your ex-wife. How many women are there in the world called Alice Casteret? That's too much of a coincidence. Not that I can begin to understand that strange business between you and Alice, about you changing her name and getting her to impersonate the real Alice.'

'She told you all that?'

'All I know is the girl in the photo is Keef's ex-girlfriend. He knew her mother, Vivienne, an old flame of Foster's. He said he thought at first that she'd died here'

'Vivienne died here?'

'*No! The model!* Alice.'

'The model died here! In this House?'

'He thought she had died. But now he's convinced that she and your ex-wife are one and the same person.'

Alex laughed. 'He's taken too many drugs I'm afraid. It would make Franco Harold Foster's grandson! It's ridiculous.'

'Which brings us round to Franco. Why didn't you go and see Keef yourself when he started badgering Alice? And why didn't you tell Franco you actually knew Keef? Remigio's lying in a morgue as a result.'

'That's Cottesloe's fault, nothing to do with me. What a tragedy. And how come you identified him?'

'And what of Harold Foster? Flying here in a panic and dying as a consequence?'

'Cottesloe again. He's a one-man disaster ... I'm beginning to wish he had drowned after all. But you shouldn't have been dragged into that crazy old rocker's fantasy world. I kept my mouth shut because I wanted to protect you from the fall-out from his false claims. I was also struggling with the impact it has had on my ex-wife. She has quite serious nervous problems, you may have noticed. That Remigio has drowned is going to destroy her ... let alone Elena. I must contact them.'

'Keef is also in very deep trouble ... '

'That's his problem.'

'It could also be your problem,' she said. 'But I'm finding communicating with you exhausting and depressing. I'm going.' She rose and Alex stood up too.

'I thought you were here to help me?'

'I was helping with the funeral. Once the ashes are scattered it's over as far as I'm concerned. I also think Irene should know a little bit about that painting,' I said and headed for the stairs, but he followed me.

'Don't rush off,' he said. 'I do need your help, not least with Elena and Alice. I don't know what I'm going to say to them.'

'I'm sure I couldn't help at all. I've met them only briefly. I don't know why I'm mixed up in all this.'

'You can't avoid it. You're a witness, you identified Remigio. They'll want you to make statements.'

'I already have.'

He checked his phone. 'There's nothing from Franco. The police will have told Elena now. Maybe Alice is with her. I must go and see what I can do. I'm going to Mazzorbo. If you won't come then you could tell Irene I'm tied up with some family problems in case she asks for a progress report. Do me that favour. I can drop you off at the landing stage of your hotel. We can use my boat – it'll take a fraction of the time it takes on a vaporetto. It'll take a couple of minutes.'

Stella said. 'Okay. Just hurry up ... '

13

WHEN ALEX APPEARED AT THE FRONT entrance of the House ready to go he had an old sports bag slung across one shoulder. We turned away from the Lagoon and walked in silence along the Calla Michelangelo towards a jetty on the far side of the Giudecca. A stormy sky had cleared and a golden afternoon sun hung just above the horizon.

We reached the moorings and Alex pointed to a sleek, teak-wood boat with a canopy covering the steering wheel up front and a hard-top covering the section behind. Once on board, he stowed the bag in a locker at the rear before taking hold of the boat's controls. I sat alongside him.

The engine coughed into life and we headed out onto the Lagoon following the shoreline that would take us around the Giudecca island and back down to the Giudecca Canal. As we passed San Georgio Maggiore, however, we were confronted by an enormous cruise ship the size of an apartment building that was about to enter the main waterway.

Alex swore and veered away, heading eastwards away from our destination. 'Those things make me nervous,' he shouted. He was looking queasy now, sweating profusely as the rolling and buffeting from the wash of larger boats took its toll.

141

Then without warning, he said, 'Take over! Quick!' and grabbed my hands and fixed them onto the wheel. I shouted out that I couldn't drive a boat but he'd already eased past me and was leaning over the side to be sick.

'Just follow my instructions,' he said, glancing back. 'Keep this side of those bricole ... ' he gestured towards the series of wooden poles that jutted up from the surface of the Lagoon and which led away into the distance, 'You must navigate on the side where the poles are numbered ... I'll tell you when to change direction, just keep out of the way of speedboats and ferries ... '

His advice meant nothing to me. All I could see was an immense stretch of water ahead as we moved further and further away from the main island.

'We're going the wrong way,' I called out. The familiar Venice skyline was soon nothing more than a grey, silver lining behind us. Clouds raced by above and we entered a grey-on-grey twilight zone. Soon, the water-traffic had diminished to just the occasional motor-boat speeding past us in the opposite direction. I wanted to call out to someone but what use would it have been? I watched as if in a dream as the sharp bow of the boat cut through the glassy surface of the Lagoon. It felt as if we were travelling to the end of the world and I felt as if I was disappearing, being swallowed up in a bad dream.

'This isn't taking us to Mazzorbo,' I said, breaking the silence between us. 'You were dropping me off, remember? Would you mind telling me where we are heading?'

'Franco's fishing hut,' he said. 'I'm cooking fresh fish for the guests tomorrow. Irene told you to help me, remember? That's what you're doing.'

'You're going to catch fish? Now? What about Elena and Alice?'

'Just follow the bloody channel ... you'll kill us both ... '

A mist had descended making vision difficult. The sun had now faded away leaving a ribbon of light across the horizon; they were moving along channels where she could see no wooden markers. Alex elbowed Stella out of the driving seat. 'I'll take over now. It's tricky from here on.'

The darkening watery wilderness stretched for miles, punctuated by natural salt marshes covered in purple grass and lined with shallow canals. Stella saw the hut and the familiar large funnel-shaped net looming up in the strange half-light. When they reached the small jetty, Alex stepped onto the landing stage and handed her a heavy torch, telling her to point it at him as he secured the boat. He then took the torch and together they climbed the short stepladder to the platform upon which the hut sat. He opened the door and switched on the light. Once inside, she saw again the cabin where Franco had brought her .

Alex switched on an outside spotlight and she could clearly see the voluminous fishing net that dwarfed the bilancia supported on its four tall metal pylons. He went to the winch switch, flipped it and the net outside plummeted, disappearing beneath the dark surface of the Lagoon. They waited in silence for what seemed an age, before he flipped the switch back and the small motor again spluttered into action. The hut hummed as the net rose from the Lagoon floor. In the spotlight's gleam, small, silvery blades of fish flipped and glinted, crabs scrambled, into the net's central cone – an elongated stocking fat with a wriggling mass of sea creatures. Stella felt sick ...

Alex pulled at a rope to shake excess water off the net and then left the cabin, descending once again in the semi-darkness to clamber into the small fibreglass coracle in which he paddled with difficulty out to harvest the haul. Stella followed him down to the landing stage and watched by the light of the fishing hut as he stood in the small craft, ducked under the dripping net canopy, undid the net tie and allowed the catch to cascade into a large bucket.

She waited with the torch as he came paddling back and helped him heave the bucket squirming with crabs, shrimps, and fish out and then up the ladder into the cabin.

'There's an ice-box in the launch,' he said, sitting down at the table. 'Could you go and get it please?' When she returned she saw that the catch was now on a large wooden draining board: crabs shifted about, claws up, searching for an exit while the soft bellies of fish slowly deflated whilst others on their silvery sides beat in frantic movements. 'The crabs go back into the water,' he said. 'Could you sort them out and put them back in the bucket?'

He rose and went back out down to the main boat, and when she next glanced up from her reluctant task she saw through the open door that he was once again out on the water in the coracle but was now struggling with what looked like a floating cage a little way along the bank. Instead of extracting fish, however, he seemed to be trying to force something down into the cage as it bobbed just beneath the surface. As she watched, he reached down to push at the thing but almost lost his balance, tipping up the small craft and threatening to capsize it.

She clambered back down to the landing stage and watched him struggle to right himself.

'You'll drown yourself if you continue like that,' she said. She held a bowl filled with crabs in her hand. As he fell back into the small boat and began paddling back, she tipped the crabs into the water. 'This really is a hateful business,' she said.

'Fish don't feel a thing,' he said, scrambling back onto the landing stage. He pushed past her, his breath now coming in heavy gusts. 'It'll be a perfect Lagoon-inspired Venetian meal.'

He sat down once again at the table and looked into the ice box where the fish still struggled. He closed the lid and stood a moment, then opened a cabinet and took out a bottle of wine. She sat opposite him. He was sweating from his exertions. 'The main course will be sea bass served with a truly outstanding risotto.'

'None of it's necessary,' Stella said. 'I'm sure she's not going to want a fish supper after scattering her father's ashes. I'm very angry at being dragged out here. I'm supposed to be with Irene and you were going to console Alice and Elena.'

He opened the bottle of wine and poured himself a glass, then took a long gulp.

'His mother is Franco's concern,' he said.

'And you could have drowned out there,' she said. 'What on earth were you trying to do?'

He proffered her a glass but she shook her head. He poured himself a second glass of wine and drank it straight down.

'I don't think Irene will thank you if you tell her about Harold and his so-called daughter,' he said. 'What difference would it make? You'll cause a lot of unnecessary trouble, simply to ease your own conscience.'

'*My* conscience – ?'

'You were right not to tell her about Keef Cottesloe in the first place. Why should you take the responsibility? Seems to me you're in a great position with Irene. She might be about to offer you a terrific job and you're flushing it away, all because of some washed-up old head-banging rocker. And what's he doing now?'

'Where Irene's concerned, I've no idea what you're talking about but as for Keef, he wants to go home when this is all settled. He's got himself a new record deal.'

'Exactly, he's famous again – that's all he wanted, publicity. If it's anyone's fault that Harold Foster died, it's his. Harold was coming here because of Keef's wild stories. And it was he who hit Remigio and probably caused his death.'

'I wouldn't drink much more, Alex. You've got to get us out of this place and back to Venice. I can't drive boats.'

As she stood up, he said, 'We're not going anywhere for a while so I'd sit down. I also think I'm coming close to having had enough of listening to what you think and what you don't think.' A wild duck grumbled in the reeds behind the bilancia. 'One thing leads to another,' he continued. 'If you tell Irene that Harold came to Venice looking for a lost daughter then you'd have to mention Keef.'

'I didn't say I was going to tell Irene anything ... '

'She's bound to discover him and that would bring her round to Alice. Alice would have to say, "I'm really someone else, I only borrowed the name and so on and so forth" ... which leads to me ... '

145

'It's none of my business ... '

'Exactly, so why am I sitting here defending myself? All that stuff about my lying to you and being responsible for people dying? All that amateur detective business with photos and who's this and who's that? You're right, it is none of your bloody business ... '

'You won't have to deal with me for much longer. Can we go now? Can we go? Alex, I need to go. Please don't drink any more. I think you're drunk already.'

He rose, giving a quiet groan as he did so.

'Stay here, I still have to sort something,' he said and he left the hut and clambered down into the small boat again.

I stood at the top of the ladder and called down and asked him if he needed some extra light but he didn't reply, just paddled a short way along the bank of the waterway to where he'd been earlier and began the struggle once again with the half-submerged wicker cage, only this time he appeared to be trying to retrieve something.

I watched him lift the cage up and out of the water and dump it onto the floor of the small boat before paddling back, his large bulk all the while threatening to capsize the tiny craft. On the landing stage, he threw the cage onto the deck of his motor launch, then called out for me to bring the fish.

I went inside, grabbed the ice-box and by the time I'd climbed down to the launch I found him tugging at a tarpaulin, attempting to cover the thing he'd extracted from the cage which now lay on the landing stage, broken and empty. There was something desperate about his movements, as if he was physically reaching a point where he might simply slump down and give up. The tarpaulin slipped and slithered and he kicked at the object beneath it and gave a cry, almost of despair.

I moved towards him and started to say, 'I can do that, you'll hurt yourself,' when he spun round, overbalanced and fell across the heap of tangled material at his feet. 'Get off,' he murmured but as he scrambled up his foot caught a rope. As he yanked to free himself, he slipped down again, dragging the tarpaulin aside to reveal the sports bag he'd stowed when we left the House.

It had fallen open, spilling its contents and by the half-light that streamed down from the fishing hut I saw a tangle of bones with a human skull attached staring up into the darkness above.

14

ALEX SAID, 'THIS IS A DISASTER, isn't it?'

Stella helped him up and, after he'd stuffed the bones back into the bag, they returned to the fishing hut.

'I must sit down,' he said. She sat opposite him as he poured another glass of wine. Outside the night had closed in, all but obliterating the horizon. He looked to Stella wearier and more bedraggled than ever but his voice was defiant, even aggressive. 'Better have the bare bones, as it were, before you run off accusing me of murder. Not a good joke, I know. I could say they're Silvia's remains out there,' he said, 'But you're not going to believe me and I can't be bothered trying anything else. You're so keen, so here we go. 'The night the model died – '

'Alice you mean – '

' – we'd all been out in the city together, except for her. Alice. She said she felt ill, that she had a cold so she stayed in the house. When we came back later, we found her lying across Harold Foster's bed, white as its sheets. "She was as still as the Lagoon ... white as the moon ... " That's from Wilde's *Salomé* ... Oscar Wilde.

'There was a panicky argument, people shouting and swearing but no one thought to call a bloody doctor. I tried reviving her but she was dead and there was nothing anyone could do.

148

'We were all in a state of shock, Foster in particular. She'd died in his bed, after all, or the one he was using. I'd met him at a party some while previously and had offered him some studio space. He'd jumped at it as it was secluded and quiet and away from the crowds. He'd worked in a small studio space up a flight of stairs from the room Alice died in.

'I don't know what had gone on between the two of them. Harold had a way with women. His technique was skilful and it relied on extreme flattery. He'd sing songs to his models while working, he'd serve champagne when they finished for the day. He was good-looking, charismatic. A secluded studio, a bed, plus she's already undressed and lying on it ... we've all been there ... so what might have happened is anyone's guess and I wasn't asking.

'To be frank, he was a serial predator of dysfunctional teenage girls, so I gather. He fathered various children by different mothers. Did you know that? You know nothing about him, do you? You should do by now. He was almost animal-like in his behaviour. He simply took what he wanted. He did whatever he liked, whenever he liked, and expected others to go along with it. I don't think he was in any way aware of it but the usual social codes that we apply to ourselves quite naturally never applied to him. He was completely amoral. That helped with the situation I found myself in.

'I told everyone to leave and that I'd deal with it. They had to be gone before I called the police and an ambulance. Everyone present had something to lose.'

'That's what Keef told me,' Stella said.

'Why was I being so generous, taking on the responsibility for a dead girl? Because of the House. I'd been sucking up to the de Maria family for two, three years, trying to persuade them to put it on the market. To have embroiled them in a sordid controversy like a young girl dying on the property after an orgy (which is what it would have looked like, let's face it) would scupper all that.

'I already had a criminal record back home in England as well as here in Italy, from the early days, nothing serious. If an enquiry into Alice's death went public, if drugs had been found, I might have been asked to leave the country. Who knows? Then where would I have gone? Back to England?

Nothing there for me. There was too much to lose so Alice had to vanish instead.'

'If you have a young, dead girl on your hands, what are you supposed to do? Wrap her up in a blanket and wait for the right moment to dump her in the Grand Canal? But she needs to be dressed in order that whoever finds her thinks she's died falling into the canal. Do you dress her or has rigor mortis set in? Do you take her body across the Lagoon and just dump her anywhere? It's not exactly Piccadilly Circus out on the Lagoon, but what if you're seen lurking about? Pushing something overboard? You'd be surprised at how public that wide open sea is! And even if I'd tried to dump her in the Lagoon, she'd have risen again, just as she's doing now, and she'd have been found somewhere. I couldn't even take her somewhere else and bury her. The burial islands are littered with skeletons but they're also swarming with archaeologists, sightseers, environmental agents ... people like you.'

'Did I have the nerve to cut her up? Absolutely not! She had to vanish but I realised that she had to somehow stay with me. That's where Mario di Maria comes in. He was an interesting architect. He liked hidden cupboards and spaces, floorboards that slid away to reveal chambers and cavities. I'd discovered one by accident when replastering some of the walls, a column that had been built into a corner of the bedroom, the one decorated with plasterwork angels and curlicues you saw the other night. Originally it had been intended as a fireplace, I think. It was the perfect sarcophagus. So, I placed Alice inside.'

Stella heard herself say, 'It's called an ossuary, not a sarcophagus.'

He looked up, as if startled that she was still sitting there.

'Whatever you call it. I wasn't to know it at the time but there's a chimney stack directly above it that serves as a vent. The smell,' he said, 'simply went upward.'

'You apparently already know about the "re-christening" of Karen. It was simple enough. I had to reinvent the model Alice. If, as was likely, enquiries were made concerning her whereabouts, the trail would lead back to the House and me. The police might have come looking, might have searched the place. But if 'Alice' made appearances elsewhere in the city *after* the date she died, then the search for her would move on and away from me.

'Karen was perfect. She was already running away from things, broken home and family. She thought it was amusing to be someone else. That's why she'd already adopted a name, Mystery something. Another name was just another twist. She never knew why I'd offered her the chance to *become* someone else, of course. She didn't know a thing about the girl she was replacing, either. She thought it was all an invention, a sort of performance art.

'I didn't tell any of those who'd been involved that night about what I was doing. What would have been the point? The real Alice's mother, Viv, wasn't going to make enquiries because she had her own problems back in England and was already under the impression that her daughter was dead. Foster simply erased the episode from his mind, as far as I could see. The others who'd been in the House were either too high or too selfish to be bothered. I didn't know Keef Cottesloe and the model were an item until he turned up this year.

'And it worked! The world moved on outside and no one noticed! I'd actually created someone from nothing. It felt immense. I would say to people in the city who'd met her, "This is Alice," and they would all say, "Ciao Alice! Come va?"

'I lived in the House with the real Alice concealed in that space behind the wall for almost twenty-five years before I ventured to take a look at her again. It had troubled me at first that I could move about the house, live a normal life close by a corpse, but I got used to it. Then, one drunken evening, sometime after I'd finally secured ownership of the House, I opened it! I didn't think there would have been much left of her by then, probably more clothing than body, some bones, maybe. I had no idea, but I took a look. I have to say, it fascinated me. Somehow, a semblance of a body remained, maybe because of the lack of oxygen in that space or because of the way the ventilation worked, I don't know. There was a skull, obviously, but her body wasn't just bones. A sort of leathery skin remained, stretched and torn ...

151

'I really should have got rid of her at that point. I'd always meant to but something prevented me. Arrogance, probably. I was so pleased with myself that I'd got away with the switch, I thought I'd keep playing the game. And so, I turned her into someone else again! Silvia, Mario's daughter. In a strange sort of way, I ceased to think of her as who she had once been. Can you understand that?'

'No, I can't,' said Stella.

'You don't have to accept all this. Maybe you think I killed her? Maybe Harold and I murdered her after an orgy. Maybe there are more skeletons scattered about the house! It's possible. Then again, maybe I'm talking rubbish, but I'm not a murderer.'

Stella's throat was dry and she continued staring at him as if in a trance, staring at his sweaty face as he unburdened himself of his astonishing, disgusting secret.

'But then along comes that fool, Cottesloe,' he was continuing. 'If he hadn't turned up and told Foster his bastard so-called daughter was still alive, none of this would have happened. I told Harold it was rubbish, that she was dead but he was mystified. Who was this "other" Alice, he wanted to know?'

' – You spoke to Harold Foster?'

' – of course, I spoke to him – he phoned me when the Keef business started. He wanted to see a grave as he thought she'd been given a private, discreet, *legal* burial and I was dreading the moment when he appeared. I'd told him I could prove she was dead but it was a dilemma. To have to tell him that I'd borrowed his dead daughter's identity and given her passport to someone else began to seem almost impossible. To say I'd boarded her up and she was now a small skeleton? I think that might have been too far even for him.

'But there was something else, something about it all that did intrigue him. He remembered the painting of her that he'd been working on. He'd left it with me and I think the idea of seeing it again fascinated him. I'd never dared exhibit it or tried to sell it. I was afraid it might cause trouble down the line somewhere. I was also afraid of what he might do.

He was prone to violence, you know. So, I was trapped.

'But then, at the last minute, he died! When that happened, it came close to solving everything. Even Keef could have been bought off, but the fool had to go and push someone into a canal and become a celebrity. And then there's you.'

He stopped talking and simply looked at me. The sound of screeching seagulls drifted across the dark water. A breeze rustled the unseen rushes. For the first time that night I understood the vulnerable position I was in. The Lagoon all around us was an immense, impenetrable universe, dark and all-embracing. It was as though he and I were the only two people left alive on earth. He could push me into the waters below and let me drown and who would know?

Until now, everything that had taken place, everything that I had been told, had seemed like a grotesque story happening to others. As I strained to make out Alex's face in the gloom, I understood that I was now part of this muddled drama. I said the first and most obvious thing that came into my head.

'So why tell me everything?'

'You insisted. It's our diabolical connection, something dark and intimate that we share.' He leaned across the table to be closer to me. 'Women are very important to me. I've always needed a female to be involved in anything I do, anything serious, that is. The moment I saw you taking pictures in the square I sensed there might be something between us although at the time I thought you were Foster's latest, last, flirtation. It happens sometimes, a girl appears and she sparks something off. It used to work that way with models, I'd meet a girl and she'd become a part of my life and work. It was always exciting, always new, an adventure. Doesn't happen so much any more these days. But you were delivered to me one night by chance and you've been in my head ever since. Do you know that no one apart from Rita Hayworth has ever worn that Salome dress but you? Isn't that an amazing thing? That's why I needed you out here tonight. You're infuriating and a pain in the arse and if this was a 19th century novel, I'd

have strangled you now and shoved you where Alice spent the last 30 years. But –'

'So that's what happened to her?' I managed to say.

'You're twisting my words. Fatti maschi, parole femmine – Facts are male, words are female ... stick to the facts.'

He rose to his feet. I also stood up. He approached me and I saw something in his eyes that caused me to step back. It was the strangest sensation. For the first time in my life, I felt that I was about to die. He said, as if reading the shock in my eyes, 'I'm not a murderer. You needn't be afraid. Really. Telling you everything means you're involved. It's a great relief. A release.'

I was ready to hit him if he stepped any closer but then he said, as if the idea had just occurred to him, 'I've got to get rid of them, the bones. I've tried to get that bag into the fish trap. It's the only place where no one will think to look but the damn thing won't sink. Could you give me a hand?'

It was such an absurd request that I could barely believe my ears. I almost laughed. From being a potential murder victim to concealing someone else's corpse in the space of a few seconds! I shook my head while trying to guess what he was going to do next. But before I could speak, a searchlight's beam illuminated Alex's face. There was the sound of a motor launch a short distance from the hut followed by an amplified cough as someone with a loud-hailer cleared his throat before calling out, 'Attention. Police. Please come out!'

Alex said, 'Say nothing. You understand nothing.'

He hurried down to the boat, waving to the oncoming police launch. I followed and as I reached his side he bent down and picked up the bag containing Alice. He turned and pushed it at me.

'She's yours,' he said. 'All yours.'

As the launch moved alongside, a policeman stepped onto the landing stage followed by second. One said, 'Guardia di Finanza Mestre.'

Alex said, 'I'm Alex Osbourne, the co-owner of the hut, collecting some fish. Do you need to see the permits?'

The second policeman ascended the ladder and stepped inside the hut without replying. He began a casual search, glancing into cupboards and beneath the table, even flushing the toilet.

'My son has all the documents. We have fishing permits,' Alex continued.

The first policeman looked at Stella. 'You are?' he said

'I'm Stella Butler,' she said. 'I'm an ecology student here on a research project. Alex gave me a ride out to take photos of the Lagoon. I'm English, I have my passport.' She placed the sack on the wooden platform, went inside the hut and rummaged in her bag, returning with her document wallet.

The second policeman glanced at her passport then reached for the sports bag. 'It's just my sleeping bag in there,' Stella said.

The man shrugged, 'Little bag?'

'Little girl,' she said. He laughed, jabbed at it with his toe, then asked Alex to go and operate the net, which he did without allowing it to dip beneath the surface for more than a few seconds. With the help of the searchlight beam the policemen illuminated the dripping construction.

They then climbed into Alex's boat and searched it. They then moved the searchlight beam across the surface of the canal, scanning the banks back and forth. One policeman climbed into the small boat and paddled to where Alex had been struggling with the fish-trap. He spent some time there before returning.

Back in the hut, the two men sitting at the small table while both Alex and Stella provided contact details. One of the men said to Stella,

'You are studying aspects of ecology in this area. Okay. You will notice several environmental violations around you contrary to the rules concerning the protection of the landscape. The toilet that discharges directly into the water of the Lagoon. The net that damages the seabed. The building resting on wooden piles that erode and destroy the mud-flats all around it.' And he laughed. 'Plenty to study.'

When they had finished, the police directed Alex to follow their launch to Mestre. I asked to be left on the Burano landing stage, and after some

155

discussion they agreed. Standing on the shore by the Burano waterbus stop, I watched the two boats disappear, the motor of Alex's boat buzzing in the gloom like a small fiend. Now I stood in the darkness in possession of a skeleton.

It seemed to me that death, both real and imagined, was pursuing me relentlessly. The feelings of anger and outrage that I had felt towards Alex had now subsided. I now felt yet another unexpected emotion. It was as if Alice now relied on me for something. She was in my care. 'Foster was a serial predator of dysfunctional teenage girls,' Alex had said. The idea that I might find a secluded spot and dump her in the water and walk away was out of the question. I couldn't leave her after all she might have been through. But neither could I wander about with her, take her on the waterbus, carry her to the hotel. That would have been madness. I was afraid that someone might stop me and ask what it was that I was lugging about.

What would I really be able tell the police? I could be seen to have perverted the course of justice. I hadn't been honest about what I knew. Alice needed to know the truth, that was certain. I thought, if I told her what I knew, that there really had been another girl, and that the skeleton was all that remained, she and I could go to the police. The real Alice would be given a proper burial. It seemed the thing to do. I called Alice but there was no answer. I texted, 'So terribly sorry about Remigio. Am coming to your house in Mazzorbo. It's very important.'

From the Burano landing stage Stella took the main path leading to the bridge, crossed over and followed the canal-hugging pathway before finally she stood looking at the blue-painted building and its lightless windows. All around her there was a dank stillness as though after a flood. The night sky seemed to rest in the water, hardly a reflection, appearing more like a dark metallic shell.

She rang the doorbell but it echoed through what appeared to be an empty house. The door was locked. She walked along to the side of the house and saw a narrow alleyway that led to a small back yard. A wooden shutter at one of the windows of the house had come away and was hanging half off. Nearby, a rusting bedstead was propped against the wall like an impromptu ladder. She dragged it across and positioned it beneath the window, clambered up onto it and reached up to try and force the window. It opened and she tumbled forward into the house. Inside, she stood and listened. There was a sound of gulls wheeling overhead outside.

She fumbled around to a doorway and found a light switch, calling out, 'Elena? Alice?' She retrieved her rucksack and the sports bag from outside, then found the main room where she and Elena had sat eating. The fire was still burning but now low and almost out.

She sat down and placed the bag on the floor, reached for the zip and slowly opened it. Inside was a small skeleton, almost structurally sound in spite of some of the bones being cracked and broken. Parts of it were covered by a strange, wizened leather-like skin similar to an Egyptian mummy's shrivelled shroud suggestive to Stella of some long-drawn-out agony. Through the open jaws of the skull she could see a double row of blackened teeth, one of which, just as Keef had suggested, was gold.

I was surprised at myself for feeling no fear, looking at the sad remains. I tried to imagine them as a girl, Alice Casteret: Keef's girlfriend, Karen's alter ego; Irene's stepsister, Harold Foster's abandoned daughter: so many possibilities crammed into a sports bag. I zipped it back up.

If I had been aware of the silence that surrounded me back in Burano then the weight of it I felt when sitting alone in Elena's house almost crushed me. The excitement I'd felt on entering soon passed and I was then seized with a sudden doubt of myself, of my strength of mind, of my character. I felt invaded, physically and emotionally. How had all this happened, I asked myself. Why had I gone back on my resolve to tell the truth? What was I doing here in this house?

I climbed the stairs that led up to the small empty bedrooms. Elena's radio was no longer on and I stepped out onto the tiny balcony off the landing that looked out over the Mazzorbo canal, leaned on the railing, and gazed into the black void of the waters beneath me. It was a starless night, dense and impenetrable, and I could only just make out the line of derelict houses on the opposite bank. I was startled by the cry of a passing bird, heading out across the distant mudflats. It seemed for a moment that I was alone in a dead world. Only a lone flashing light from a small boat approaching before receding in the darkness or the nearer sound of the dip of an oar in the water hinting at hidden canals and nocturnal journeys suggested otherwise.

I went back inside and waited, wrapped in an old coat I had found. I felt I had to see this through. I turned on a small wall light and I could see a silk canvas hanging on the opposite wall on which had been embroidered two large tuberoses set in a pattern of scattered dark hexagonal shapes with a deep red border. It was like being a child again, miserable and unable to sleep. I tried to lull myself into dreamland by counting the shapes over and over again, restarting each time I was distracted, once by distant church bells chiming the half hour, then by the sound of birds scrabbling on the tiles above me. Eventually, I found myself counting church bells, then birds, before I fell into a dark, dreamless sleep ...

How long I was unconscious I have no idea, but I awoke quite suddenly, my heart already beating painfully against my ribs, as if I had somehow sensed danger while still asleep. I listened, aware that something had changed, but was unable to see anything at all. I fumbled for the wall-light and flicked the switch. As the soft light disseminated itself over the room, I realised I was not alone. A human shape loomed out from the shadows, someone slumped in a chair a few feet from where I was sitting. I heard myself gasp in fright as my chest constricted and my heart seemed to stop. I'd never felt such a sudden pain and thought I was going to faint as the sharp jolt to my system had left me speechless and paralysed. I waited. The woman did not move and as the minutes passed I regained my composure. My heartbeat resumed; my breathing became regular once again. I then took take a closer look at the woman, who must have stolen into the room as I slumbered. Her head lay back over the chair and her face was turned up to the ceiling, her eyes closed as if she was wrapped in a deep sleep. It was Alice Casteret ...

Prompted now by a mounting sense of concern, I looked closer. Was she sleeping? Or had she fainted? She was breathing regularly, but with deep heavy gasps, and at certain moments she clenched her teeth as if experiencing some kind of mental spasm.

She was sweating and I reached out to touch her forehead as she bunched her fists and contorted herself, writhing where she sat.

'Alice!' I said. 'Wake up. What's happened to you?' She didn't respond, so I grasped her by the shoulder and shook her. 'What have you done?' I said and slapped her face but still didn't succeed in rousing her. She was in a coma of some sort, insensible to sound, insensible to touch.

I reached for my phone and, in a voice I failed to recognise, tried to call an ambulance. At the same instant, Alice raised herself, opened her eyes, and looked upward. I let out an involuntary cry of fear and recoiled as she shuddered and appeared to convulse again before letting her hands fall to her sides and slumping back into the chair. I ran from the room.

15

DAY SEVEN: SATURDAY

VENICE LAGOON. OSSARIO DE SANT'ARIANO

THE NEXT FEW HOURS PASSED IN a whirl of confusing images and sensations. A water ambulance arrived, siren screaming, blue lights flashing, illuminating the nocturnal canal. Paramedics resuscitated Alice before taking her out to the waiting craft, wrapped in blankets and semi-conscious. I, too, was given a blanket and I sat with her as we sped through the darkness to the Lido, where we were transferred to a motor ambulance and driven to a drug-recovery unit. I sat in a corridor, wrapped in my blanket, falling in and out of a half sleep, interrupted by nurses who offered me coffee. At around 6 am. I was awoken by someone prodding my shoulder. It was Franco.

'What are you doing here?' He didn't sound very friendly.

'Alice and I were going to meet at her house on Mazzorbo. She didn't arrive, but I went into the house and fell asleep. She woke me ... How is she?'

He sat down beside me. 'She's fine. The police told her about Remigio yesterday afternoon. I tried to contact her but she had disappeared. Alex will be here soon to take her back to the Giudecca.'

'Where's Elena?'

'With family here on the Lido. They've charged your friend Keef with Remigio's murder. He's admitted hitting him. The police say they were fighting over money which they'd both stolen.'

'That's ridiculous. It was money Alice nd Remigio raised, selling Elena's

160

lace, wasn't it? Alice told me that Remigio was angry about it. You must tell the police it wasn't from a robbery.'

'The murder charge will amount to nothing. The police feel foolish that they went public identifying the wrong man. I know them. I've told you I'm not inclined to help him. None of this would have happened if he'd left my mother alone.'

'Keef got it wrong where your mother was concerned but the person he was searching for did exist. Alex knows it. I don't think you do.'

'I must get back to Mazzorbo and see what kind of mess the police have made of the house. They're looking for drugs! She OD'd on sleeping pills but they're convinced there's a hidden pile of cocaine or something. What did they ask you?'

'I haven't spoken to the police, just a doctor.'

'You look a mess. I could drop you off on Burano, it'll be quicker for you. I must collect some things for my mother to take to Alex's. She's being transferred there today. She won't be going home for a while.'

We left the hospital and were soon heading back across the Lagoon. It had occurred to me that if the police were searching the Mazzorbo house they might find the skeleton. I felt resigned and almost relieved. When we arrived, Franco went ahead of me into the house but when I joined him the sports bag was still where I'd left it on a bench. The police, apparently, had not left a mess.

'Let's get on,' he said but I then made another decision. I said, 'I was going to show your mother something last night. I'll show it to you.'

I took the bag, laid it on the ground and opened it. Franco glanced at the skeleton and laughed.

'Typical! The police turn the place upside down searching for drugs but overlook a dead body! How the hell did that get here?'

'It's been here since last night. Alex had tried to dispose of it at the fishing hut before giving it to me.'

'Alex did what?'

'We went there to collect fish for the meal at Alex's, for Irene's guests later this morning. We were disturbed by Lagoon police ... '

161

'He told me about the police. I warned him not to go out there at night showing lights ... '

'Alex was trying to get rid of this skeleton. It's what's left of a girl called Alice, the girl Keef mistook for your mother. The original Alice.'

'That's Silvia. He's had it around the house for years.'

'Alex told me that she was Harold Foster's daughter. She died from a drug overdose after a party at his house and that he'd hidden her body away in order that everyone, including him, could go on with their selfish lives. He hid her in the cabinet in the wall in one of the bedrooms. Something prevented her from disintegrating completely.'

'These are a child's remains. It's too small for a woman. And she wasn't hidden away ... he showed her to you. I've seen it, too. Many years ago.'

'He didn't intend that I saw her last night. That was a mistake.'

'You really mustn't believe everything he says, you know ... '

'Why would he waste an hour of his life spinning a yarn like he did?'

'He's an arch fantasist. It's part of his charm, his weirdness. He can't resist a drama. It's the vanity, the homburg hat concealing the bald pate. He was spinning a yarn. He likes to invent things, likes to shock people. He was probably hoping to frighten you into bed. He's taken a fancy to you.'

'He wasn't spinning a tale, he was confessing ... '

'Confessing! Alex?'

'Keef told me the same story, almost word for word. The girl OD'd and everyone in the House left in a hurry. Your mother told me about her adopting a new identity at Alex's suggestion although she didn't know who she was replacing. Your mother's real name is Karen. And then there was Harold, coming here because Keef said he'd found his daughter. Alex was anxious about it because of what he'd done to this girl. Or not done.'

Franco continued, 'Foster wasn't coming back to see a real girl. He was coming back to see the painting. Girl on the Bed. Do you know what it's worth? Getting on for £2m. Alex has provenance but Foster began to cast doubts on that. Alex was worried about Foster's interest in the painting, not some mythical daughter.'

162

'Is that what Alex told you? So why were you bribing Keef?'

'Keef was pestering my mother, driving my mother mad.'

'She'd begun to realise she'd replaced a dead girl. She'd been trying to keep all this from you and probably Remigio. She was afraid for you, and now she's lost Remigio ... '

Franco stood and tapped the bag with his toe.

'You say Keef came here working on the theory that his girlfriend was still alive. Correct?' he said.

'Yes.'

'And that's why he was pursuing my mother. He thought she was his ex-girlfriend. He wasn't looking for a dead body.'

'The original Alice's mother Viv told Keef she was still alive.'

'Back in 1970 or whenever all this was supposed to happen, did Keef see a dead body?'

'No.'

'And, when telling you all this, did he mention my father or the house?'

'He couldn't remember the house, nor Alex – but ...'

'So Keef left Venice forty years ago after a girl he knew suffered a drug overdose, in someone's house, somewhere in Venice. He wasn't sure whose house it was or where it was nor whether she was actually dead.'

'But there's a photo of Keef and the model. I have it here and your father's in the background. He knew the model, Alice, he knew Keef, and he knew Harold.'

Franco looked at the photo. 'I can't see a dead body anywhere. As for my poor mother, she can't be relied on for anything to do with her identity. She just claims she's someone else! She knows nothing of anyone dying. Alex is the only one who's suggested that someone died but there's no corroboration of his 'confession'. As for this' – he indicated the photo – 'I'm quite sure there was a model and that many people passed through my father's house. It was a boho existence. But none of that means that this thing in the bag is a girl who might have dropped dead and whom my father might have hidden away until she rotted. This thing is Silvia, de Maria's daughter, the child who died. How did you end up with it?

'I told you. When the police arrived at the hut, Alex shoved it into my arms.'

'You know why he did that? I told you earlier. Handling old bones in Venice is an offence. He gambled on the police not asking to look in your bag. He was in enough trouble as it was. And why didn't you tell the police what you had?'

'I was very confused. There are so many people involved. Other people's lives ... not least your mother's ... '

'You did nothing because the whole tale is just garbled junk emanating from Keef, who is now facing an actual murder charge. This is just a pile of old bones. What's your real interest in all this? Why are you busying yourself in other people's lives like this?'

'It's the other way around. Ever since I arrived here, people have been telling me things I didn't need or even want to know. But I'll try one more time. You say this is not the model Alice, that it's a relic and has nothing to do with Keef. But, just supposing it is Alice, then that would mean Keef was on the right track. If there had been a girl, Alice, the one Keef was seeking, who died and whose body your father concealed as he said he did, whose identity he stole and used to give your mother a new identity as he and she said he did, then where would that leave you?'

'Leave me?'

'Alex sent you off with lots of money to try and get rid of Keef but he didn't tell you the real reason for doing it. He left you in blissful ignorance because he wanted to pay Keef off and get rid of him, not because of your mother's health but because Keef's persistence was leading everyone to poor little Alice here ... very inconvenient for him.'

Franco shook his head.

'You told me you haven't any family on your mother's side, that she had a strange childhood and never knew her parents. That's because she took this girl's identity ... or was given it by Alex. The point is, thanks to Alex and in small part your mother, you don't even know who you really are.'

'I know exactly who I am.'

'Do you? I think if someone had deceived me like your father did for so many years, I'd be extremely upset. And annoyed ...'

Franco shrugged. 'It comes with the territory.'

'Why not take the remains to the authorities and have them identified? That will establish whether this is Alice, or Silvia, or some poor wretch who died in 1600 or something from the plague. Everything flows from that ...'

He remained silent.

I pressed on, 'And if it really is Silvia, why hasn't he told the family who sold him the House? Wouldn't they be interested?'

Franco seemed to think for a moment, then, 'My own theory, for what it's worth, is that he got this thing from a dealer, someone who'd stolen it from one of the islands around the Lagoon. There are places knee-deep in these things. Everyone in Venice has a corpse hidden away somewhere. They turn up in canals, in cupboards, on deserted islands. They're digging up thousands of them all the time. The place is a stinking graveyard where the bones never settle. You should know that; you're studying the ecology. You saw Mario's pictures were littered with images of skulls and bones.

'But it's a very serious offence nowadays, you can't remove and disturb remains for ecological reasons. And things have suddenly changed for Alex. The art-world, the serious art world in the form of Irene Foster, has arrived at his door and he's revelling in it. She has plans for the 3-Eyes. He probably felt nervous at having this pile of bones hanging around when the place might be the scene of previews and exhibitions and the like. He thought he'd dump them. As usual, though, he made a bloody disaster of it ... '

He rose and picked up the bag. 'Silvia belongs to Alex. It's his responsibility. I'll return it, her, to him. Come on, you must get away from here. Back home where you belong.'

We boarded his boat but instead of heading back across the Lagoon towards Venice, he turned away and sped in the opposite direction. My heart sank. Franco said, 'I want to check on the fishing hut. He'll have left things in a mess. It won't take long ... '

In silence, in crisp morning sunlight, we made our way through twisting-turning, unmarked channels interspersed with large tracts of saltmarsh. I felt desolate. Everything smelt, of decay, of polluted waters; the aircraft roaring away from Marco Polo airport in the far distance seemed louder, somehow.

That we were not even heading for the fishing hut became clear when the walls of the island of Sant'Ariano loomed into view. There was a sense of inevitability about everything. As we drew nearer, Franco said, 'There's a problem with the engine ... ' and it duly coughed, spluttered and then died. He cursed quietly as the boat silently drifted towards a jetty.

'Could I borrow your phone?' he said, 'Mine's out of credit. I'll call someone to come out. It won't take long.' She handed it to him just as the boat touched the jetty boards. 'No signal,' he said.' He tied up before stepping onto the rotting structure. 'Wait here,' he said, leaping down onto the shore. She saw he had the bag containing Alice's remains slung over his shoulder. She watched everything happen as if in a daze. He hurried away following the line of the perimeter wall and as he disappeared round a bend, she fumbled with her camera to take a parting shot. It was a futile, weak gesture, she knew.

There was only silence now, broken by an occasional banging, crunching sound that seemed to come from over the island wall. The little boat rose and fell on the greasy surface of the channel waters. Time passed and she shivered. She looked back out across the Lagoon, now bleaker and more featureless than ever. It really was just mud and water. She checked her watch. He had been gone for twenty minutes.

She stepped onto the landing stage. There was a tall gate-like structure some hundred yards along from the jetty. She passed a large white sign that proclaimed, Ossario de Sant'Ariano. As she approached the gate, it opened and an overall-clad worker stepped out. Startled, she stopped and he slammed the gate to. "Non ormeggiare. Vietato!"

She turned and set off in the opposite direction, along the litter-strewn, slimy foreshore, tripping on bunches of muddy reeds. When she reached a break in the wall, she clambered to the top of it and searched for signs of life. There was nothing to be seen but a thick mass of tangled bushes growing everywhere.

She jumped down and fell forward into a deep ditch, scratching her arms and face on a mass of thorny brambles. She rose and stumbled forward, her feet encountering large stones, shattered earthenware, fragments of terracotta tiles. When she reached a point where she could see above the dense green jumble of shrubbery she was confronted with a bleak landscape of overgrown farmland and deserted buildings. She knew it was her imagination, but there seemed to be a terrible gloom hovering about the place. She caught a brief, distant glimpse of tilted tombstones; she turned and through a break in some small trees she caught a glimpse of Franco standing, looking down. She scrambled towards him.

As she drew near, she could see that he was stamping on something; she knew it would be Alice's skeleton. He turned as she approached and he shrugged, then stamped down hard. There was a cracking sound and she saw the torso was being reduced to splintered shards. 'Don't Franco, please!' Stella said and reached out to grab at his shirt. 'It was just wrong to stuff her body away for all those years and let it shrivel and not give her a proper burial. There was no dignity to it. But this is disgusting. I think she deserves a little respect ... don't you think?' but he pushed her off, and said, 'It's nothing to do with you. Nothing.' He grabbed a handful of the shards and moved off, scattering them in the undergrowth, stamping on them as he did so. The sports bag remained and she saw Alice's skull protruding. He returned and said, 'Go away, go,' and he knelt to take out the skull. As he did so, there came a shout close at hand. It was a workman with another man close behind. The workman waved his arms and yelled, "Vietato! tenere fuori! si deve lasciare immediatamente! si deve lasciare immediatamente!

Franco stood up, holding the skull. He then looked down at it, swore and tossed it to one side into some small bushes. He then advanced towards the approaching men, holding his arms out wide as if puzzled. Stella held back and as the men met, she thrust her hands into the bushes and grasped the skull.

I shoved it into my rucksack before striding away, leaving Franco in deep conversation with the men who were gesticulating at the ground. When I reached the boat, I sat in the stern and waited. He arrived half an hour later looking flustered and pale. Without a word, he started the engine and we headed off towards the Lagoon. When at last he spoke, his tone of voice was unpleasant, defeated but gloating. They had questioned him. He would be reported to the police. A trespasser accused of stealing bones! The irony! The empty sports bag lay on the boat's floor. 'It's all going to be levelled; the whole area is being flattened. As will Silvia be, or whoever she was,' he said.

I said nothing, waiting for him to ask for the skull. I braced myself for a struggle but he seemed preoccupied with manoeuvring the boat through channels and out into the open Lagoon. In the confusion, I realised he hadn't seen me pick it up.

'I'm protecting my mother,' he said at last, as if I'd asked him something. 'The risks are too high.'

As I stepped off the boat at the docking-point on Burano he said: 'Go home,' and he tossed my phone across the boat at me and we watched as it clattered onto the concrete steps. 'Just disappear and mind your own business.'

I sat on a bench from where I could look out across the Lagoon, my head throbbing, blood drumming at my temples. From somewhere unseen came the incessant rumbling and clanking of a dredger. Small heavily laden industrial barges passed across my vision; faces of workmen on board turned towards me but I was concentrating hard on the whirl of contradictory thoughts which filled my head.

In the rucksack Alice's skull rested against my spine; it was absurd, I knew, but the protective urge that had propelled me over the Ossuary wall to snatch it from Franco still animated me. It was as if Alice herself rested like a child in a sling, sleeping, and it was my responsibility to see that she received some kind of justice after all these years. Franco wanted to obliterate her, finally remove her from the world. His impatient denials and scorn for the truth were merely echoes of what had occurred in the Tre Oci all those years ago.

168

But what to do? Where to go? Taking the skull to the police was not an option. Where had I found it, they would ask? What could I prove? Turning it in somewhere like a piece of lost property was also impossible, while casting it into the water would be worse than what Franco had in mind. It – she – had to be returned to where she'd rested for thirty years. Quite why, I had no clear idea, only that I had to do it. The rest would take care of itself, in some way. As I rose, I said to Alice, 'We'll have to take you back, I'm afraid. There's no other way ... '

16

I GOT BACK TO THE MAINLAND AND to my hotel in time to watch the scattering of Harold Foster's ashes on Veneto TV in my bedroom. It proceeded as we'd planned it. The ashes casket was situated beneath a gilt canopy on a richly decorated water-hearse boasting gold statues of angels on either end. Irene sat in the stern along with friends and family; smaller water taxis followed the flower-decked hearse as it made its outlandish way towards the sea beneath a wide, cloudless pale blue sky. It was a perfect day for a scattering. The glassy surface of the water was disturbed only by the ever-widening ripples caused by boats and ferries criss-crossing to and from the Lido.

When they reached the designated spot, Irene and Seth leaned over the side of the hearse pausing a moment for the cameras, before tossing the pink and red cylinder overboard followed by a wreath. The launches rose and fell on the swell as a priest standing alongside Irene intoned his blessing over the gradually disintegrating canister.

Afterwards, I spent a couple of minutes booking myself onto an evening flight home. I then left the hotel, leaving my newly bought working outfit folded neatly on the bed. Half an hour later, I was stepping off the vaporetto outside the House with Three Eyes, my rucksack on my back, but without a clue as to what to do next.

The main front door was open and I climbed the familiar staircase to the main studio room where guests were already gathered. Almost immediately Irene rushed towards me. I expected her to be angry, to ask where I had disappeared to, to wonder why I wasn't wearing my new clothes, but she was in a world of her own.

'Wasn't it inspirational! We've scattered Harold's ashes, a beautiful, solitary moment out on the Lagoon ... and you were such a big part of all that! And now we're here! My God' and she hugged Stella close.

Minutes later, seated on a chaise longue in the studio and clasping Stella's hand, Irene gazed about her, chattering loudly. 'What an uproar!' Irene laughed into Stella's ear. 'But you're really pale, Stella, what a strange look! Are you okay?'

'I'm fine. It's been a long morning ... I want to ... '

Irene broke in, again surveying the room, 'Harold would have loved this place! It feels like his spirit has returned to somewhere that was important to him, don't you think?'

As guests approached and greeted Irene, she introduced each one to Stella in turn: 'Stella, this is Michael, chief art critic of *The New York Times* and, Wow! Philippe! This is Philippe, *the* Manhattan dealer ... and this guy! He's director of the Guggenheim in Venice.' The latter shrugged and smiled. 'Stella's going to work for us in London. You'll be seeing a lot of Philippe ... ' She turned to Stella, a sly smile on her face.

'Stella,' she said, drawing herself closer, 'I must tell you something very important. I'm flying home to New York tomorrow. Seth is staying here, settling some legal affairs, but you'll be thrilled when you know that I'm putting money into this place, Alex's beautiful House. I just love this place ... it's like a magical palace. Tre Oci – what a name! Harold's work can be exhibited here.'

'Harold Foster's work in this place, here?' Stella managed. 'But ... '

'It's going to be magnificent! And I want you to be a part of it!' and she gripped Stella's wrist. 'No, no, hear me out. You've been a miracle. You believe in "serendipity"? It's my guiding philosophy. That's you! You

171

happened here like a small miracle. We stumbled upon one another because of Harold, and you led me here! It's all falling into place! I want you to work for me permanently because it's so *right!*'

Just then Seth appeared and gestured to Irene. She said to Stella, 'Stay here, I must speak to someone. Don't go! Stay where you are!' As Irene disappeared through a distant door, Stella also rose.

Music drifted overhead as she eased her way past chattering guests. Dull winter sunshine seeped through the tall studio windows; although it was mid-morning, lights had been turned on and the House seemed to Stella to be bathed in a premature twilight. She had seen nothing of Alex as yet but knew he was busy somewhere nearby, watching her. He would have heard from Franco, would imagine Alice's bones had been destroyed. She felt the rucksack against her back, and almost smiled.

Then without realising it, she found herself standing in front of the small painting on a easel. The inscription simply read: Girl on a Bed by Harold Foster (1975) (Alex Osbourne). On a table beside it were a pile of photocopies.

As I stared at the painting, my eyes filled with tears and for a moment I was blinded. It took me completely by surprise and I stood hoping that no one would come and stand next to me and try and talk to me. I wiped my tears away with one hand and picked up one of the photocopies with the other.

I was angry for Alice. Whether she was Irene's half-sister, Keef's groupie girlfriend, Vivienne's errant daughter or just some lost soul washed up on Harold Foster's grubby bed, she was now irrelevant and disposable as a person. She was an event.

As if he had somehow tuned into my thoughts, Alex appeared close by, and without looking at him, I could tell he was watching me, wondering what might be about to happen. The inevitable homburg hat sat askew on his head, a carnation in the buttonhole of his dark suit jacket and a glass half-filled with champagne in his hand. Large dark sunglasses concealed his eyes.

A small group of guests gathered around him, and he began to deliver a lecture. I'd heard it before of course, almost word for word:

'The relationship of painter to sitter is a paradoxical one of intimacy and detachment, exploitation, conspiracy and friendship. It's always been my contention that, as a life model, you stand somewhere between 'high' and 'low' culture, between nude and naked, between art and pornography.' There was some laughter from the guests.

'Some people say my own work teeters on the knife-edge between the ethereal and the erotic.' There was some laughter from the group. 'Saint or sinner?' Alex continued, and winked at me. 'As artists, we tread a fine line. Harry Foster's oeuvre was dominated by the naked model but he always said that his paintings were a sort of self-portrait. "They're all autobiography," he once said to me. 'So, what's the story here, then?'

He turned to face me as if challenging me. People stared at me. I was about to speak, to say something, although I hadn't the faintest idea what. He stepped towards me, reached out and embraced me, hugging me tightly. 'This is Stella, everyone. She's responsible for arranging this event and for bringing Harold Foster's daughter here. She's also a fine model!'

There was a tiny ripple of applause as he released me but held me at arm's length as if wary of what I might do next. His apparent disdain for me and what I had witnessed the previous evening shocked me. I saw that he was sweating, and he smiled at me.

I said, 'I came to say goodbye. I'm catching a plane this afternoon.'

His mouth opened momentarily before closing again. He turned to the small group watching and said, 'Excuse us for a moment,' and we moved to a quiet corner of the studio. I had no idea what I might say next. It was as though I was floating.

'I'm so glad you came back!' Alex said, his voice cracking, sounding throaty and weary. 'And I'm very sorry you were put through all that angst last night.' Was he referring to Alice's attempted suicide, I wondered, or what had happened at the fishing hut? 'And I'm glad we're not parting on bad terms. I owe you a lot.'

'Me?'

'Of course. Without you there would have been no Irene.' He leaned closer so that I could see his small eyes behind the dark glasses, 'Irene's going to buy into the House. She wants to help convert part of it into a gallery for Harold's work. Here, in Venice! My debts will be wiped out, it's like a dream come true. It was you who led me to her.'

'Serendipity,' I said. I wondered to myself why I hadn't slapped his face or screamed at him. Alice's skull was pressing into my back. I realised I must wait for something from him to latch onto, to work with.

He continued talking, 'We had a good night, didn't we, when we danced together, when you whirled for me! That's what I'll remember about all this.'

'I'd never whirled in public before. I enjoyed that evening, despite your lies.'

'I'm still carrying the scars,' he said and laughed. He paused a moment as if turning something over in his mind. 'Talking of Salome,' he said, 'I want to give you something. Wait, don't go away.' He left the room, returning within seconds cradling an oblong box under one arm. He opened it with his free hand.

I knew, even before I saw it, what it would be. It was the Rita Hayworth Salome dress that I'd worn the night I'd danced. He proffered it to me.

'I'd like you to have this.'

'You're giving me Rita Hayworth's dress?' I said.

'Everything, the earrings, the ring. They're all yours.'

'But you paid a lot of money for these things. You're a devotee. You don't want to give them to me.'

'You looked great in them, the perfect fit. As I looked at the Salome dress in its box, the inkling of an idea was forming.

I said, 'It's a crazy thought, but as it'll be the last time you see the dress, couldn't I put it on again? One last time. Everyone would be thrilled. Irene would be over the moon. You could play "Sadie Salome" on the piano ... '

Somewhere beyond the room where we were standing, Alice was struggling for her life, Keef was facing a murder charge; Remigio was lying in a morgue, Elena was stricken with grief and I was suggesting I dress myself up like a 1950s film star. Alex pushed his dark glasses back onto the crown of his head. His eyes were bloodshot, his face sweaty.

'You'll put it on?' he said in disbelief. 'Don't answer that, you might change your mind! I'll go and tell them ... to set it up ... You're not trying to pull a stunt?'

I laughed. It was such a relief. A stunt! Of course, it was a stunt!

'I'll need somewhere to change. I can't change here,' I said. 'I'll need to see myself in a mirror. I'll use my room, the one where I slept. I know the way,' and I took the box from him and set off. He followed and as we entered the familiar bedroom I thought of something else.

'Can I take a photo of you,' I said. 'Here. You don't mind, do you?'

He stared at me without expression as though trying to see beyond my words, and for a moment I thought I'd overstepped the mark. He gave a tiny exasperated sigh but went and stood by a window.

'No, by one of the caryatids,' I said.

'Hold on,' he said, and leaned on one of them, reached for his hat, tilted it to one side, puffed out his chest and stuck one hand into his jacket, Napoleon Bonaparte-style. I took the picture and as it wound itself through he came close to me and leaned into me as if to see the result.

'Go, quickly and I'll join you,' I said and pushed him away. He grasped my hand, bent forward and kissed me lightly on the cheek. He said, 'An Italian saying: 'Vento, tempo, donne e fortuna – prima voltano e poi tornano, come la luna. Wind, time, women and luck – first they turn away and then they come back, like the moon', and he left hurrying away down the corridor.

In the bedroom Stella stood before the familiar caryatids and tried to recall how Alex had opened the cavity. He had pressed against the forehead of one of the figures and the hearth had opened at his feet. She pushed in similar fashion but nothing happened, nothing gave way. The one on the left! she suddenly recalled him saying. She pressed and the forehead gave way. She heard the creaking sound as the hearthstone turned revealing the bicycle pedal attached to the wheel. She went to the bedroom door, listening for sounds of anyone approaching. Piano music drifted up from the studio. She closed the bedroom door.

Back at the hole in the floor, she knelt down and began to push the pedal. It was stiff and she had to use both hands to achieve any purchase but as much as she rotated the circular mechanism, the wall-panelling that had opened that distant evening remained unmoved, unyielding.

Minutes passed and she felt herself growing hot with the effort, her hands becoming slippery with sweat. She pushed again and again and had almost given up in despair when there came a creaking, splitting, sound. She looked up to see the wall panel suddenly spring open. It had been jammed. The pedal now turned easily and the dark cavity that had been Alice's sad home for thirty years was revealed.

She rose and pulled open the rucksack, grabbing at the skull. As she lifted it towards the gaping hole, her sweating palms lost control of the smooth surface of the bone and it fell, bouncing down onto the rug and rolling away into a corner. As it tumbled, Stella noticed something spin off, a tiny gleam of light, and disappear beneath the bed.

Stella grabbed the skull again, placed it inside the cavity before fumbling in her rucksack to retrieve her camera. She took a picture of the gaping hole with the skull sitting inside it before sliding back onto on her knees to frantically rewind the pedal until the aperture closed. She then pressed the caryatid's forehead and the hearthstone slowly closed.

Falling onto her hands and knees, she looked under the bed and spotted a thin little dental plate attached to which was a small gold tooth. As she reached out for it, someone behind her said, 'What are you doing?'

I looked round, startled. Alice was standing at the door. She was dressed in loose-fitting pyjamas and had a bandage wrapped around one arm. She looked as if she had just woken from a bad dream. I stood up, bewildered.

'What were you doing, opening that thing?' she said. She stepped into the room, went across to the bed and sat down. 'What's that?' She indicated the dental plate in my hand. I looked at it as if it was the first time I'd seen it.

'I'm getting changed,' I said. 'I'm modelling for Alex. He wants me to dress up as Salome. Earrings, bangles. You should be in bed, you're not well.'

'You're not a model,' Alice said.

'No, I'm an amateur,' I said. 'You look very tired. Let's get you into bed,' and I took her hand and helped her stand up. I then pulled the covers of the bed back and said, 'Come on, jump in. You must sleep.'

She lay back down and I pulled the covers over her. I stood at the foot of the bed for a moment looking down at her.

'Have I had an accident?' Alice said. 'I've no idea how I got here.'

I waited until her eyes had closed, then I took out Elena's lace fisherman and placed it on the pillow beside her.

From below came the sound of Alex's piano. I walked along a corridor and stood by the staircase that led down to the studio and listened. Alex was talking to the people gathered below, presumably waiting for my grand entrance.

'This is an Irving Berlin song about a Jewish boy upset at finding his nice, Jewish girlfriend playing the infamous Salome on stage. Mose, the man in question, goes to the theatre to watch her perform and is horrified to find that Sadie, his girl, has become a stripper. The song made the real stripper Fanny Brice famous. We're hoping for the same career boost tonight! It's called "Sadie Salome, Go Home!".' He began to sing,

'Sadie Cohen left her happy home
To become an actress lady
On the stage she soon became the rage
As the only real Salomy baby'

As he continued, I moved away, found a door that opened onto another staircase that I knew led down to the courtyard, by-passing the studio. As I opened the front door of the House I could hear the assembled guests joining in the chorus,

'Don't do that dance, I tell you Sadie
That's not a bus'ness for a lady!'

I then made my way out of the House and into the open air.

SITTING IN THE LA PALANCA CAFÉ further along the Giudecca quayside, I ordered a coffee and took out the box containing the Rita Hayworth dress. I wrote a brief note to Irene, thanking her for all she'd done and apologising for having to hurry away. I then wrote her name and the address of the Bauer Hotel on the lid. I turned out the contents of my bag, scattering snaps and objects across the table and assembled a pictorial narrative: a cutting from an Italian newspaper announcing Foster's death; a card displaying Alex's gallery; then a photo of the House with Three Eyes; a cutting announcing Keef's 'death'; Keef's photo of the studio taken in the House with the original Alice and himself, Harold and Alex in the background (I ringed Alex's head in biro); my photo of the same studio wih the same view across the canal; the photocopy of the Foster painting of Alice on the bed; a photo of the bones lying in the sports-bag; a photo of Alex standing in front of the caryatids; and lastly a photo of the open cavity in the wall. I then took out the dental plate with the gold tooth attached and placed it with the rest of the items in a stout brown envelope. On the envelope I wrote the address of the police-station where Keef was being held, plus Keef's name and that of Donato Berenga and sealed it.

I opened the box containing Keef's drum-beating bear and placed him on the table in front of me. As I did so, the café proprietor looked across and said, 'Bene! What's he do?'

I wound the bear up and we watched as he twirled, tapping his little drum, tap, tap, tap across the counter. I said, 'Would you like it?'

'Si!'

'I'll do you a swap. I'm leaving tonight and I won't have time to post these packages. Could you do that?'

He said, 'Of course. Va bene ... '

I handed over the box and the envelope and he put them on a shelf behind the counter. He then took the bear and placed him on the counter. 'What's his name?' he said.

I thought for a moment, then said, 'Mario.'

The man laughed. 'Super Mario!'

When the vaporetto arrived at the Palanca stop, I hurried to the front, found a seat amid a clutch of tourists and watched as the Giudecca shoreline fell away behind us in the evening light. Soon, I could just make out the House, its three main windows blazing with light. I held my camera up to take a last snap but as I did so a German tourist craned round to take a picture of his girlfriend, obscuring my view. There was a swirl of wind, rain and spray, and when he sat back down, the Giudecca and the House with Three Eyes had disappeared.